LORD OF THE DAWN

Lord of the Dawn

The Legend of Quetzalcóatl

Rudolfo Anaya

UNIVERSITY OF NEW MEXICO PRESS
ALBUQUERQUE

First paperbound printing, 2012
Paperbound ISBN: 978-0-8263-5175-3
E-ISBN: 978-0-8263-5191-3

18 17 16 15 14 13 12   1 2 3 4 5 6 7

Library of Congress Cataloging-in-Publication Data
Anaya, Rudolfo A.

Lord of the dawn.
1. Quetzalcóatl. 2. Aztecs—Religion and mythology.
3. Indians of Mexico—Religion and mythology. I.
Title.
F1219.76.R45A5   1987   299'.78   87-16219
ISBN 0-8263-1001-X

Design: Milenda Nan Ok Lee

Contents

Introduction

Quetzalcóatl: Myth, Legend and History

David Johnson

*T*he stories and traditions surrounding the figure of Quetzalcóatl, the Plumed Serpent, form one of the most important cultural legacies of ancient Mexico. At one time his influence stretched from what is now Guatemala to northern Mexico. Even after the repression of native religion by the Spanish the reputation of Quetzalcóatl continued to grow. Because of his admirable spiritual ideals, Quetzalcóatl was thought to be the apostle Saint Thomas by early Spanish friars. Others saw in his white hair and beard a European adventurer, a Norseman or Irishman, or perhaps even a sage from Atlantis. Whatever his origins, Quetzalcóatl's legendary stature has continued to intrigue and influence thinkers and writers century after century. Beneath the difficult names and foreign trappings of his tradition are universal themes which engage our common humanity and stir the imagination.

I

The mythology of any culture is an expression of its spiritual, psychological and social backbone; it is *sacred history*. Obviously, I am not using the word "myth" with its current connotation of falsehood or fantasy, but with its traditional meaning of those stories from around the world which describe the creation of the world by a god (or gods) and the creation of animals and humans, stories about heroes and heroines which define the parameters of human existence and establish meaningful attitudes towards the basic mysteries of birth, puberty, marriage and death—irrespective of "scientific" truth or falsity. Myths embody the universal quest for the purpose of life, and the desire to decipher the enigmas of transcendent powers. The best stories provide models for the exigencies of daily existence.

The first difficulty, however, of dealing with Mexican mythology and the figure of Quetzalcóatl is the relative scarcity of information. In some respects, we know more about the city of Athens 2,000 years ago and the Hebrew Kingdom of David 3,000 years ago than we know about the Toltec Empire on the Mexican plateau 700 years ago—though that picture is slowly changing with the growth of archeological evidence and the study of ancient manuscripts.

Information is scarce because Spanish friars immediately following the Conquest attempted to eradicate the native, "pagan" religion by destroying the written books or codices of the Aztecs and Mayas. Although the hieroglyphic style of the pre-Conquest Aztec books was too simple to record a written literature, the books were used as invaluable mnemonic aids for an extensive body of oral literature memorized in their schools. Only sixteen of these books still exist: three of them are Mayan and six are from the Oaxaca region. In the remaining books there is some evidence of Quetzalcóatl's role as a wind god who descends from the Dual-God above (Ometeotl) and creates the earth by lifting the heavens.

Most of our knowledge about a pre-Conquest culture, other than archeological evidence, comes from post-Conquest scribes and scholars. Ironically, Spanish priests also became the primary collectors of whatever native materials survived—the most famous collector was Fray Bernardino de Sahagún. The priest-ethnographers enlisted native wise men who apparently had access to extant pre-Conquest books, and using the Latin alphabet they recorded in Nahuatl the ancient myths, sagas, prayers, chronicles, songs and speeches. Often these documents have Spanish or French glosses. In addition, there are early letters and histories written by Spanish settlers. These materials gathered dust in various libraries and museums in Europe and the Americas, and were largely forgotten until the turn of the century when scholars began to edit, translate and interpret them for a wider public.

A God of Creation

Quetzalcóatl was a very old god who was originally associated with shells, sea and wind, and probably had his beginnings along the Gulf Coast. The *quetzal* forming the first half of his name is a rare and precious bird with long tail feathers used for ceremonial dress, symbolic of the powers of the sky and the aspirations of the spirit. *Cóatl* means "snake" or "serpent" and is tied to the energies of the earth, the mysteries behind fertility and cyclic renewal. Thus in *quetzalcóatl*, the "plumed serpent," ancient Mexicans had discovered a composite figure that combined spirit and matter, or mediated between them, reconciling the two realms of heaven and earth. The Plumed Serpent's name was Kukulcan in the Yucatan and Gucumatz in Guatemala. The Green-Feathered Serpent was known as far north as New Mexico and southward to Columbia, Peru and Bolivia. The Winged Serpent can be also found in European folklore, but its most emphatic kin are found in the Orient, the Chinese Dragon and the genii of rain and fertility.

Quetzalcóatl's oldest role in mythology was that of a creator deity. The ancient Mexicans, like the Native Americans of the Southwest and the Hindus of India, believed that the cosmos had undergone several cycles of creation and destruction prior to this one. The first four ages or Suns are similar in the several creation accounts, and roughly correspond to the four basic elements of the cosmos, and of life itself: earth, air, fire and water. Although sources differ in the ordering of these ages, a commonsense pattern might begin with a water world ruled by the goddess of water, Chalchiuhtlicue, when people were

fish, and proceed through evolutionary stages to the
ages of monkeys and giants. Each age was sustained
by a delicate balance between opposing forces, dra-
matized in the myths as a titanic struggle between
the gods Quetzalcóatl and Tezcatlipoca. It was not,
however, a struggle between good and evil, such as
we might find in a Zoroastrian or a Christian version
of history, but a question of harmonizing or balanc-
ing the antithetical powers of light and dark, day and
night, sky and earth, spirit and matter (as in the Ori-
ental conception of *yin* and *yang*). Disharmony or
disproportion brought destruction and the end of an
age. This world view is graphically shown on the
large Aztec calendar stone in Mexico City. From the
Codex Chimalpopoca comes this description of the
present or fifth age, called the Sun of Motion (*Ollin-
tonatiuh*):

> The Fifth Sun with its sign 4-Motion is called the Sun
> of Motion because it moves according to its own path.
> Thus the old ones say that under this Sun there will be
> earthquakes and hunger. And when this happens we will
> perish.[1]

In another creation story Quetzalcóatl and
Tezcatlipoca created the heavens and the earth by
tearing in two a monstrous earth goddess. Afterwards feeling badly about the harm they had
brought her, they gave her gifts and created the
mountains, caves, trees and flowers from parts of her
body. The story concludes: "This is the same goddess

who sometimes weeps in the night, longing to eat human hearts. She refuses to be silent if she is denied them, and she won't produce fruit unless she is watered with human blood."[2] This goddess became the basis for the popular Southwestern story of La Llorona.

The principle of opposition, which produced the cosmos, originated in Ometeotl—the androgynous, supreme god of duality. Described as both male and female, day and night, life and death, earth and sky, Ometeotl's dual nature produced four sons, who, as the four quarters of space, were transformed into the four ages. Unquestionably, this is an elegant and elaborate mythic model for dramatizing dynamic change and cosmic evolution.

In addition to his role in the cosmos, Quetzalcóatl was a culture bringer, the discoverer of agriculture and the fine arts of working with feathers, jewels and clay. He invented the sacred calendar. One of Quetzalcóatl's most important tasks was the creation of man and woman after the earth had been stabilized. It was necessary for Quetzalcóatl to descend into the underworld where he was put through a series of tests and trials by Mictlantecuhtli and Mictlancihuatl, Lord and Lady of the Land of the Dead, who were reluctant to give up the bones needed to create the new generation of humans. Finally, Quetzalcóatl returned with the bones which were ground up, fertilized and transformed into human beings.

Like the descent myths in ancient Greece and Babylonia, Quetzalcóatl's archetypal journey into the earth suggests the analogy of human life to the vegetation cycle, pointing to the primordial idea that the source of both life and death is in the underworld—a place not to be confused with the Christian hell. Quetzalcóatl provided food for humans by changing into a black ant and raiding Tonacatepetl, Food Mountain.

Creation myths like these provide the groundwork, a kind of blueprint of the cosmos and its origins: how did it all begin and how does it all work? The stories reveal the origins of human beings, food, fire, suffering, death, religious rites, as well as any other ingredients essential for material and spiritual survival. The book of Genesis laid such a foundation for Judaism and Christianity. The writings of Hesiod and Homer served a similar function for the Greeks. The Mexican creation myths portray a serious concern with time, perhaps an obsession with it. Their myths provide the dates for deities involved with previous ages, as well as causes for their demise. The sacred calendar or almanac, the *tonalpohualli*, details the various gods and attendant powers controlling the hours, the days, the months and the years. This was necessary for divination and the observance of religious ceremony. But there was also the added concern about the end of the age. The inevitable destruction of the present age, the Fifth Sun, by earthquakes is reflected in the profound fatalism of Aztec and other Nahuatl-speaking poets. Nevertheless, the end could be postponed if, with sacrifice and penance, the Sun were kept alive and healthy in its passage through the sky. This belief provided a purpose and divine mission for the Aztecs as "Warriors of the Sun."

The Worship of Quetzalcóatl: Priest and Ruler

Very little is known about the details of Quetzalcóatl worship prior to the ninth century, although it is believed that Quetzalcóatl played a major role from the third to the eighth century at the great ceremonial center of Teotihuacán, the "City of the Gods". At the height of its power, Teotihuacán was possibly a city of some 200,000 people, with broad economic and political influence over the region. As a sacred city it was built according to a cosmic design reflecting the integration of deities and mortals: a central axis called the Pathway of the Dead by archeologists connects the soaring pyramids of the Sun and Moon at one end with the Temple of Quetzalcóatl at the other. This axis is crossed by the East-West avenue, which in effect quarters the city, making it compatible with the deities of the four directions and of the four prior ages. The smaller palaces and pyramids, the numerous workshops for art and artifice, the lovely frescoes and carvings, point to Teotihuacán's cultural importance. Undoubtedly, there were schools that trained the children of nobility for positions of responsibility, and spread the spiritual teachings and practices of Quetzalcóatl. The ceremonial areas were burned about A.D. 750 and its influence waned, but nevertheless it continued to serve as ceremonial model for later urban centers.[3]

The Toltecs, who inherited the culture of Teotihuacán after its decline, dominated central Mexico until the twelfth century. They were primarily the descendants of Nahua-Chichimecs who had migrated from the northern plains in the ninth century, spoke Nahuatl, and formed the basis for a common culture in the Valley of Mexico. The name Toltec means both a "master craftsman," and an inhabitant of Tollán, the legendary city of their mythology located at the center of their world. Tollán probably refers to what is now called Tula, where the central pyramid was dedicated to Quetzalcóatl as the "morning star". At an earlier time Tollán might have been located at Teotihuacán.

A cult surrounding Quetzalcóatl flowered in the tenth century with the Toltecs and mythology became intertwined with history, producing a legendary lineage. The name Quetzalcóatl was associated with the messianic rise and fall of a Toltec culture hero, ruler and priest, Ce Acatl ("One Reed"—his birthday) Topiltzin, who is perhaps Mexico's first historical figure of record. Topiltzin's father Mixcoatl, the legendary leader of the Toltec-Chichimec tribe, was murdered by his brothers and immediately elevated into a tribal deity. Topiltzin's mother was either Chamalma (who became pregnant by swallowing a piece of jade) or Coatlicue (the powerful earth-goddess). Very little is known about Topiltzin-Quetzalcóatl's childhood except that he trained as a warrior and defeated the uncle who had earlier killed his father.

When Topiltzin became a priest of Quetzalcóatl and a ruler in Tula in the tenth century, his life and destiny were blended with the cult traditions of the Plumed Serpent. Topiltzin-Quetzalcóatl, for example, was credited with founding agriculture and feather working, as if he were the incarnation of the primordial deity, even though the Toltecs had obviously inherited these skills from earlier civilizations. He was credited with the accumulation of wealth and power by the Toltecs: with huge ears of maize, and squash two meters in circumference, with vast treasures of jade, turquoise, coral, silver and gold.

In addition to the material and artistic benefits represented by his reign, Topiltzin-Quetzalcóatl became a spiritual model for his people, advocating a life of self-discipline, learning and piety. Apparently Topiltzin-Quetzalcóatl's spiritual practices, his opposition to human sacrifice and his deep piety, alienated a rival, militaristic faction that favored human sacrifice. A deep rupture was created in Toltec society, which eventually led to the exile of Topiltzin, and ultimately to the destruction of Tula and the Toltec dynasty in the twelfth century.

Another prominent ruler linked to Tula and this period of history was Huemac. Scholars either place Topiltzin and Huemac at the two extremes of Tula's existence, beginning and end, or make them contemporaries, with Huemac being instrumental in expelling Topiltzin-Quetzalcóatl from Tula. Then Huemac himself was expelled, eventually hanging himself in the Cave of Cincalco, near Chapultepec. Afterwards he assumed the Kingship of the Underworld, not unlike the famous Minoan King Minos of Knossos.[4]

But it is the story of Topiltzin—his fall from power, his pilgrimage to the sea, his death and resurrection—that provides a magnificent drama of the human spirit and reaches epic heights of beauty and power. Leaving in disgrace, but promising to return, this hero-priest journeyed to the east in fulfillment of his destiny. The circumstances of his fall open a number of windows into the culture and consciousness of the Mesoamerican.

Quetzalcóatl's Fall, Death and Resurrection

An account in the *Anales de Cuauhtitlán*, a mixture of myth and history, states that at the height of Toltec fame and prosperity the high priest Topiltzin-Quetzalcóatl withdrew from society, withdrew into the privacy of his temple where his vassals protected his privacy. Several times before, sorcerers representing a militaristic faction in Toltec society had attempted to undermine his power because of his opposition to human sacrifice and warfare, and his belief that the only sacrificial offerings should be tortillas, snakes, flowers, incense and butterflies. In the year *Ce Acatl* (One-Reed) three sorcerers tried again. Their leader was named Tezcatlipoca, Quetzalcóatl's mythic, primordial adversary, with whom Quetzal-cóatl had created and destroyed the four earlier ages. Tezcatlipoca's clever plan was to bring Quetzalcóatl out of seclusion, get him drunk, and thus subvert his priestly, ascetic vows, forcing him into exile.

Disguised as a servant, Tezcatlipoca, whose name means "smoking mirror," used a mirror (probably made from obsidian) to get Quetzalcóatl interested once again in his body. The mirror itself raises questions about self-knowledge, narcissism and a healthy balance between flesh and spirit. When Quetzalcóatl saw how emaciated he had become, he resolved to stay hidden from society, but the sorcerers made him a beautiful ceremonial outfit out of quetzal feathers and a mask out of turquoise. A second look in the mirror and he was ready to come out of retirement. The sorcerers then prepared a savory stew from herbs, tomatoes, chile, green corn and string beans. Then to satisfy Quetzalcóatl's thirst, they brewed a batch of pulque mixed with honey. Quetzalcóatl and all his personal servants became drunk. He then requested the presence of his sister, Quetzalpetlatl ("mat-woven-from-quetzal-feathers"), who was performing penance on Mount Nonohualca. Although incest is implied in the text, there is also the connotation of rebirth, as if the ascetic priest must become fully carnal, fully immersed in the flesh, before he can abandon Tula and begin his journey to death and resurrection.

The next morning after the drunken party and the

breaking of penitential vows, Quetzalcóatl and his followers realized that they had lost the contest with the sorcers and must abandon their kingdom. Quetzalcóatl lay down in a stone coffin where he died a symbolic death of the old life. After four days he emerged reborn, ready for the final stage of his life. Leaving behind all the finery and riches of his reign, he traveled simply, without riches, a typical pilgrim. At one point his only companions were dwarfs and cripples, signifying his abandonment by the high and mighty of Toltec society. He left important signs along the way, sacred marks or shrines for local worship. Evidently, the journey represents the spread of the cult of Quetzalcóatl, from Cholula to Chichen Itza in the Yucatan, where his name became Kukulcan. The fact, however, that human sacrifice became so popular at this Mayan ceremonial center, suggests that a different charismatic leader was involved, and *not* the former pietistic priest from Tula.

According to the myth, Quetzalcóatl traveled to Tlillan Tlapallan, the "land of black and red." Geographically this might be in Campeche, Tabasco or western Yucatan, but its mythic location was the eastern horizon—where the morning star announces the rebirth of the sun and where the *red* sun leaves the *blackness* of night. Symbolically, it was the place of spiritual fulfillment and enlightenment. One version of Quetzalcóatl's end is provided by Sahagún who depicts Quetzalcóatl leaving on a raft of serpents. This version is related to Quetzalcóatl's mes-

sianic promise to return one day from over the
water. Unfortunately, the text itself is truncated and
plain.

Jesvs?

When he arrived at the seashore he made a raft of serpents. He got on this raft, sat down and used it like a
boat. And thus he left, navigating across the sea.[5]

The second version from the *Anales de
Cuauhtitlán* describes in poetic prose Quetzalcóatl's
arrival at the seacoast and his ceremonial end.

They say that in the year One Reed, having arrived at
the sacred shores of the holy sea, he stopped and wept.
Then he gathered up his vestments and dressed himself
for a ceremony, putting on his robes of quetzal feathers
and his turquoise mask.
When he was finished dressing, he immediately set himself on fire, and was consumed by the flames. For this reason the place where Quetzalcóatl was burned is called
Tlatlayan (Burning Place).
And it is said that as he burned, his ashes rose, and all
the precious birds appeared, rising and circling in the sky:
the scarlet guacamaya, the blue jay, the lovely thrush, the
shining white bird, the parrots with their yellow feathers,
and all the other precious birds.
When the ashes were gone, at that moment, the heart
of Quetzalcóatl rose upward. They knew he had risen
into the sky and entered the heavens.
The old ones say that he became the star that appears
at dawn. They say that it appeared when Quetzalcóatl
died, and because of this they named him Lord of the
Dawn.[6]

With this grand finale Quetzalcóatl fulfilled his destiny in several ways: first, as the masked god, the plumed or winged serpent; second, as the phoenix, a universal symbol of rebirth and immortality; and third as the morning star, which signifies in its periodic cycles Quetzalcóatl's own death and resurrection. In addition to his reconciling role between heaven and earth, between matter and spirit, it is the transformation of his spiritual pilgrimage into images of amazing beauty and resonance that places him in the select company of mythological heroes. ♥

Conclusions

The figure of Quetzalcóatl was so important to ancient Mexico that it caused two momentous cases of mistaken identity, first with the Aztecs and then with the Spanish.

At the end of his journey, Topiltzin-Quetzalcóatl, in a messianic manner, promised to eventually return and redeem his city of Tollán in the year *Ce Acatl.* Several years prior to Cortés' actual arrival, the Aztecs experienced several astronomical and terrestrial events which seemed to predict a future catastrophe: Lake Texcoco boiled, and such phenomena as columns of flames, comets and a man with two heads were seen. The Aztecs feared for their magnificent island capital of Tenochtitlán, the most recent recreation of the legendary Toltec capital of Tollán.

Through an incredible coincidence, a possibility

occurring once every fifty-two years, Cortés and his
band of conquistadors arrived on the shores of Mexico in 1519, the year *Ce Acatl* in the Aztec calendar.
Such was the power of the Quetzalcóatl myth—and
the impact of unsettling omens—that the Aztec
rulers believed initially that the Spanish were Quetzalcóatl and his retinue returning to claim the
throne. Cortés' ships were reported to Moctezuma II
as floating mountains or perhaps Quetzalcóatl's four
mythic temples (built for penance and symbolizing
the four directions). This mistake contributed to
Moctezuma's strange passivity and his indecision
about defending the Aztec capital. The Aztecs, who
had followed destiny and the warrior god
Huitzilopochtli out of the wilderness into a promised
land and political hegemony, were conquered. In less
than two years their world was decimated.

The case of mistaken identity for the Spaniards re-
sulted from Quetzalcóatl's reputation as a pious
man, and the possibility that he was, in fact, the
apostle Saint Thomas, who was supposed to have
evangelized the East Indies. Although the first Fran-
ciscans after the Conquest repressed native religion,
by the seventeenth century writers and priests had
collected evidence showing the similarities between
the cult of Quetzalcóatl and Christian practices: such
as the rites of confession, communion, baptism and
penance. Crosses were discovered throughout Mesoamerica, along with miraculous springs, and the im-
prints in stone of Quetzalcóatl's hands and feet.
Sixteenth-century scholars like Fray Diego Duran

said that Topiltzin-Quetzalcoatl's life and his red beard reminded him of Saint Thomas. Sahagún described Quetzalcóatl with a miter, surplice, sandals and a shepherd's crook—similar to a bishop's staff. Finally, in a famous sermon of 1794, the Dominican of Monterrey, Fray Servando Teresa de Mier, reviewed the evidence and concluded that indeed Quetzalcóatl was Saint Thomas. Don Carlos de Siquenza y Gongora, a famous writer of the period, called Saint Thomas-Quetzalcóatl the Phoenix of the West.7 ♥

Although his religious influence diminished in the nineteenth century, the figure of Quetzalcóatl remains an exemplary hero from ancient Mexico, a model of all that is admirable in Nahua culture, in contrast to the sometimes bloody, oppressive picture of Aztec society. Modern scholars like Laurette Séjourné, Octavio Paz and Miguel Léon-Portilla have explored Quetzalcóatl's historical and philosophical importance. John Bierhorst, J. H. Cornyn, Arthur J. O. Anderson, Charles Dibble and I have translated the myth. Writers like José Lopez Portillo, Archibald MacLeish, Tony Shearer, and D. H. Lawrence have recreated the myth for modern audiences. The most recent addition to the Quetzalcóatl canon is Rudolfo Anaya's most imaginative *Lord of the Dawn*.

Irene Nicholson points to the riches that can be discovered in the figure of Quetzalcóatl: "In so far as he is symbol, he presides like the wind over all space. He is the soul taking wings to heaven, and he is matter descending to earth as the crawling snake; he is virtue rising, and he is the blind force pulling man down; he is waking and dream . . . Quetzalcóatl is time itself, the serpent, yet paradoxically he exists beyond time."[8] Altogether the many masks of Quetzalcóatl celebrate the most important dimensions of our mortal condition: from the origin of life in scales and shells to the heroic pilgrimage towards the flowering and fulfillment of the human spirit. And finally into the shadowy recesses of death and the yearning for rebirth.

Notes

1. Translated from *Anales de Cuauhtitlán*, in the *Codice Chimalpopoca*, ed. and trans. by Primo F. Velázquez (Mexico City: Imprenta Universitaria, 1945; 2d ed., 1975. As a measure for Velázquez's edition and translation, I used Walter Lehmann's German and Nahuatl edition, *Die Geschichte der Königreiche von Colhuacan und Mexico* (Stuttgart und Berlin: Verlag von W. Kohlhammer, 1938). The English translations in this introduction are mine, and were first published as complete stories in *Puerto del Sol* (Volume 21, Numbers 1 & 2).

2. Angel Maria Garibay K., *Épica Náhuatl* (Bibl. del Estudiante Universitario, No. 51. Mexico City, 1945).

3. See David Carrasco, *Quetzalcóatl and the Irony of Empire* (Chicago: University of Chicago Press, 1982).

4. See Nigel Davies, *The Toltecs, Until the Fall of Tula* (Norman, Oklahoma: University of Oklahoma Press, 1977).

5. Fray Bernardino de Sahagún, *Historia General de las Cosas de Nueva España* (Mexico, D. F.: Editorial Porrua, S.A., 1979), Bk. III, Ch. XIV.

6. *Anales*, Velázquez (note 1).

7. See Jacques Lafaye, *Quetzalcoatl and Guadalupe: The Formation of Mexican National Consciousness 1531–1813*, trans. Benjamin Keen (Chicago: University of Chicago Press, 1976).

8. Irene Nicholson, *Mexican and Central American Mythology* (London: Paul Hamlyn, 1967).

One

*L*ong before the Spaniards came to México,
Lord Huémac ruled in the ancient city of
Tollán, the capital of the Toltec Empire. At
that time the Toltecs were the most powerful nation
in all of central Mexico. Lord Huémac had gained
control of the city through his cunning and his al-
liances, but there continued to be much dissension
and agitation. Many factions continued to oppose
his rule as Lord Huémac was a harsh ruler. From the
provinces which surrounded the land of the Toltecs,
numerous groups of Indians sent their warriors to
test the strength of Huémac, and in Tollán the wise
men who extolled peace, opposed Huémac's con-
tinual wars.

Lord Huémac allied himself with the Jaguar Cult,
a group of warriors, which he kept armed and at war
in order to consolidate his gains and to retain his
power even though his military adventures were
costly, and the people suffered. Since Huémac
schemed and conspired and repeatedly broke his
pledges and promises, he forfeited the allegiance of

many of the groups of the Toltec Empire. To retain
control he pitted group against group, and his harsh
laws and edicts created much civil unrest and dissension.

When the people of Tollán gathered at the marketplace, they complained of the harsh rule of
Huémac. Though the wars of Huémac brought many
slaves and much tribute to Tollán, the wealth was
used to keep the Jaguar Cult and the Eagle Cult
armed and at war. Old neighboring groups became
enemies, and the peace of the Toltecs was no more.
The people wept as they remembered the ancient
prophecy which foretold that the sins and transgressions of an unprincipled ruler would bring ruin on
their sacred city of Tollán. The people whispered and
complained but they were powerless. Even the wise
teachers and advisors of the city, the tlamatinime as
they were called, turned away from Huémac and
spoke against him.

"I curse the philosophers and the priests!" Huémac
shouted at his Captain of the Warriors as they stood
in the courtyard of his palace. "I am the Lord of
Tollán! I am the ruler of Tula! I make the laws, not
the priests!"

Huémac looked at his Captain, then turned to
look at his daughter and his wife who were sitting in
the shade of a ceiba tree. They sat weaving cloth of
cotton and quetzal feathers.

"My Lord, do not curse the wise men of the
Toltecs," his wife said. "They are the teachers of the

Ancient Word, they guide us in the true way of the Toltecs."

"They have no right to judge me!" Huémac bellowed. "They would turn the people against me. They are weak men who do not understand that for Tollán to remain strong, I need many warriors!"

His wife shook her head. "But warriors are only one small part of our society," she said. "The Ancient Word tells us that the tlamatinime and the priests are entrusted to preserve the peace and prosperity of the people. They also show us the way to lead pure lives."

Huémac sputtered, picked up his bowl of pulque and drank as he resumed his pacing. His Captain spoke to fill the silence.

"Many of the priests have supported our war efforts," he said, "but it is this new priest, Quetzalcóatl, who is creating a disturbance. He tells the people that the Toltecs have lost their way. He asks them to return to art and wisdom and the path of the Ancient Word."

"Bah!" Huémac grunted. "Art and wisdom are fine, but only when your borders are secure. Farmers need more land to farm, so I enlarge the Toltec Empire. The artisans need precious stones and gold, so I bring those to Tollán. Does he understand that?"

"He opposes war," the Captain said.

"It shows how little he knows about reality," Huémac muttered. "Without my warriors the people would have nothing; there would be no Toltec Empire."

"But war for the sake of war is not right," his wife shook her head. "I have heard the priest Quetzal-cóatl speak of peace, of nobility and grandeur through wisdom and the arts. He is a priest of the Ancient Word. He has come to restore the Toltec greatness—"

"I am in charge of Toltec greatness!" Huémac shouted. "Without me and my warriors we would long ago have been overrun by our enemies! Every wandering group that appears at our borders threatens our stability. Why can't the people under-stand that? And you!" He stopped and looked ac-cusingly at his wife. "I do not want to hear you speak of Quetzalcóatl as a teacher. He opposes my law! He is insolent! I shall forbid him to show his face in Tollán!" He paused and his wife bowed her head and returned to her embroidery.

Huémac looked at his daughter. He would forbid her to listen to the teachings of Quetzalcóatl. She was a lovely young woman, soft and fragile. She was called Precious Gem, and she was a precious gem scintillating in the soft light of the sun. Many war-riors had admired her beauty and asked for her hand in marriage. I will not give her to a young warrior, Huémac thought as he gazed at her. Some day she will sit by my side.

"Do not expose my daughter to the teachings of that priest," Huémac said abruptly. His wife looked up in surprise but said nothing. She glanced at her daughter, for a moment their eyes met, then they re-turned to their work.

Huémac continued to pace. He did not feel well. The evening before had been warm and he had drunk too much pulque with his warriors. They had celebrated a recent victory against a neighboring tribe. Many slaves had been taken; including a courtesan who called herself Butterfly Woman. Huémac had taken her for himself and had provided a house for her and her women near the marketplace.

His Captain arrived with new reports which disturbed his morning rest. The neighboring Huaxtecans were complaining of the taxes Huémac extracted from them as tribute, and there was talk of waging war. Just as disturbing was the report of a tribe of people moving in from the north, the ferocious Chichimecas.

"Chichimecas?" Huémac said aloud, rolling the word on his dry, swollen tongue, as if the word itself were an omen which foretold no good for the Toltecs.

"Yes," the Captain said. "Barbarians from the north. They are a lowly tribe of beggars. They claim to be looking for their homeland. They have a prophecy, a legend which states they are destined to assume power in a place they will call Mexico-Tenochtitlán. There, they say, they will build a new empire."

"Beggars!" Huémac yelled. "Just like all the other tribes which wander about without a place to call their own. They look at us with envy. If we lower our guard they will attempt to invade the Valley of Tula. They want our land!"

"Our wealth attracts them like the nectar of a flower attracts bees," the Captain said as he glanced at Huémac's daughter.

"Yes, they want our land, our wealth. No doubt this priest Quetzalcóatl would open his arms and receive them!"

"It is our way to take in the poor and wandering stranger," his wife said softly, daring his wrath.

"Not my way!" Huémac answered. "This land is for the Toltecs. We will oppose all newcomers. We will rule Tollán forever!"

Huémac wheeled around to face his Captain. "Send Tlacahuepan to me," he said.

The Captain was surprised and annoyed, a frown crossed his brow. As the Captain of the Jaguar Cult, he expected Huémac to consult only with him, not with Tlacahuepan the sorcerer. Nevertheless, he nodded, bowed and exited. Lord Huémac's command was law.

Huémac's wife and daughter also rose to leave, retreating without a word into the quiet of their chambers. They were not allowed to be present when Lord Huémac took counsel with Tlacahuepan, for Tlacahuepan was a sorcerer, a disciple of the god Tezcatlipoca, deity of darkness.

Tlacahuepan appeared in the courtyard. "My Lord," he bowed before Huémac. "How may I serve you?"

Tlacahuepan was dressed in the attire of a high priest, in flowing robes and a headdress of quetzal feathers. He served Tezcatlipoca, one of the four deities created by Ometéotl, the father and mother of all the gods. ♥

Huémac took his sorcerer aside. "My Captain has brought me reports of new attacks on our empire. It seems I am beset on all sides. Even here at home, the wise men, the tlamatinime, refuse to swear their allegiance to me. They insist the teachings of the Ancient Word do not condone war or human sacrifice to the sun. Now I hear reports that the priest Quetzalcóatl draws the people to him, and that he is a man of peace. Tell me, Tlacahuepan, who is this priest? How does he command the loyalty of the people? From where did he come?"

"This young priest came from the eastern shore," Tlacahuepan answered. Some say he is Huaxteca, but the truth is not known. He calls himself a priest of the sun."

"The sun is the father of us all," Huémac said.

"True, but Quetzalcóatl says the sun is his father. He claims divine powers." Jesus

Huémac laughed. "Oh, another one of those! Our city attracts many of those wandering priests who claim strange powers. How is this Quetzalcóatl different?"

"Quetzalcóatl says he is a priest of Ometéotl," Tlacahuepan continued. "He says Ometéotl, the Lord of the Universe Who Created Everything for His Pleasure, is his father."

"What!" Huémac blurted. Then he laughed. Ridiculous, a priest claiming that Ometéotl, the Navel and Foundation of the Universe, is his father.

"He is a strange priest," Tlacahuepan nodded, "he cares nothing for worldly pleasures." Yes, he thought secretly, a strange and powerful priest. Quetzalcóatl had been in Tollán only a short time, yet already he had acquired a strong following. The arts he taught to the people were truly remarkable. The wise men, the nobles, the artisans flocked to him; under his guiding hand, the city blossomed.

"He calls himself a priest of the sun," Tlacahuepan continued, "but he tells the people it is forbidden to sacrifice human hearts to our Father Sun. He does not believe in blood sacrifice."

"But everyone knows the sun requires the blood of human sacrifice to move through the sky," Huémac said in surprise. "Without blood to feed its energy the sun would not rise, it would die and we would all perish."

"We know that, my Lord, but Quetzalcóatl does not believe as we do. He teaches the people that the sun requires only butterflies and lizards as sacrifice, not human hearts. It is nonsense, but many believe and follow him. They are returning to the teachings of the Ancient Word as taught by Quetzalcóatl. That is one reason why the people resist paying your taxes for war, my Lord. Quetzalcóatl has taught them that we need no sacrifices in the temples."

"I see," Huémac nodded. An angry frown crossed his face. "And why haven't I been informed about this?"

"My Lord. You have been engaged in waging the wars for the protection and growth of the empire, that is your function. Meanwhile Quetzalcóatl has worked here in Tollán, raising his temple, teaching the arts. He has worked quietly but has gained a large following."

"Why haven't you put a stop to his work?" Huémac demanded.

Tlacahuepan turned away, he was angry. He had tried to discredit Quetzalcóatl, but the young priest was too powerful. He seemed to be surrounded by a purity which kept him from harm. But now Tlacahuepan thought he could use the authority of Lord Huémac to destroy Quetzalcóatl. If Huémac was aroused, then perhaps his strength could defeat the young priest.

"Quetzalcóatl is difficult to deal with, my Lord. His followers guard him well, protect him. He claims he came from the Unlimited Divine Waters of the Eastern Sea. Many believe he is a god—"

"A god!" Huémac thundered, his ire roused anew. "No man is a god in my empire. Does he dare to blaspheme the old teachings! Send my Captain to arrest him!"

"The people protect him," Tlacahuepan repeated. "They call him Topiltzin, Dear Prince—"

Huémac grew infuriated. "There is only one prince of Tollán! Me! This man is an imposter! I will cut his heart out and feed it to the dogs at the marketplace!"

Tlacahuepan smiled. He had stirred jealousy in the heart of Huémac. Now he would proceed with caution and cunning.

"I need to repeat to my Lord that the priest Quetzalcóatl has a large following. Those who follow him devote themselves to art and knowledge. He has trained the finest artisans in Tollán. Even the wise men sit at his feet to listen to his teachings. When he came he brought maize with him; he has taught the farmers, they follow his teachings. He brought many edible plants, and he brought cotton which grows in many colors and does not need to be dyed. He has taught the builders how to construct new temples and houses and roads. As you have made war, my Lord, Quetzalcóatl has made peace. I believe he is a sorcerer, that is why he can accomplish the things he does. He is powerful."

Huémac listened closely. His rage calmed. So, Quetzalcóatl was not just a wandering poet, but a worthy opponent who had established himself in Tollán while he, Huémac, waged war in the provinces. To get rid of Quetzalcóatl now would be difficult, an act which might bring more strife and dissension at exactly the time Huémac needed the support of the people. He needed their taxes and their work to continue his campaigns. Perhaps Quetzacóatl would provide the way. If the rich nobles and artisans followed his teachings, then they would fall in step if Quetzalcóatl were in alliance with Huémac. Huémac smiled.

"It seems to me that this Quetzalcóatl is a wizard. Imagine, cotton of many colors." He laughed. "Maybe he will fashion a new weapon of war for us, a weapon so terrible it will put fear in all our enemies."

30

"He preaches against the way of war, my Lord."

"Bah. He will listen to reason," Huémac scoffed, still smiling at the prospect of having the priest pay allegiance to him.

"As I said, he preaches that there should be no human sacrifice. He preaches that the Sun accepts only flowers and butterflies. . . . "

"Then he is an idiot as well as a wizard," Huémac laughed, "a harmless dreamer."

"With many followers," Tlacahuepan reminded him.

Huémac grew serious. Yes, the city of Tollán had changed. In the city the impressive temple of Quetzalcóatl was under construction, and in the Valley of Tula, as far as the eye could see, the fields of corn and cotton grew. So the priest Quetzalcóatl was responsible for these amazing things, and many people followed him, they were eager for him to teach their sons and daughters. The people considered the calmecac, the school where the tlamatinime taught the most elevated teachings of the Toltec culture, as a wise path. But Huémac needed young warriors taught in the telpochcalli, the school of warriors.

Perhaps he had delayed too long; the situation called for quick action. He turned to Tlacahuepan.

"I must speak to this priest. Bring Quetzalcóatl to me. It is in our destiny to meet, so it shall be now."

Tlacahuepan hesitated. He had hoped to incite Huémac's anger, so that he would insist on the death of Quetzalcóatl; now he wanted to meet the young priest. This did not bode well.

"My Lord," Tlacahuepan began to protest, but Huémac cut him short.

"Bring Quetzalcóatl to me."

Tlacahuepan bowed. "I go, my Lord."

Two

Lord Huémac awaited the arrival of Quetzalcóatl with anticipation, and some trepida-
tion. His mood had lightened; the evening
was cool with the arrival of the rainy season. During
the afternoon Huémac had reviewed his warriors
and found them in top form and good spirits. They
were running races against the recent captives. The
fame of the Toltecs as runners was known
throughout the nation, and this knowledge incited
the captives to prove their own skill. Each captive
warrior yearned to defeat a Toltec in a race, but it
was a hopeless challenge.

The vendors from the marketplace had gathered to
bet on the races when Huémac arrived. The bets
grew in size, and the runners ran with more deter-
mination. Huémac added to the excitement by promising that any captive who could beat a Toltec in a
race would gain his freedom, those who ran and lost
would be sacrificed immediately. The races grew
more intense.

The Captain of the Warriors served pulque and

Lord Huémac enjoyed the afternoon. He marched
through the streets, pausing briefly at the house he
had established for Butterfly Woman. The woman
was young and lovely. It had been a good day,
Huémac thought.

Now in the cool of the evening Huémac stood in
his garden and tipped the cup of pulque to his lips. It
was good to be ruler of the Toltecs. His word was
absolute law. Let the wise men of Tollán be critical;
he was Lord Huémac, Lord of Tollán, and he would
do as he pleased. In the old days a warrior would
pay with his life if he slept with a fallen woman, so
strict was the law of the Ancient Word. But that was
the past. The present time was what mattered, and
the present time was the time of Lord Huémac. He
smiled and drank again. He remembered Butterfly
Woman. Yes, it had been a good day. He believed
things would go well with Quetzalcóatl, perhaps an
alliance could be arranged. Huémac had given orders
that he was not to be disturbed while he talked to
the priest, not even Tlacahuepan was to be present.

"Perhaps this priest is not as wise as people say,"
Huémac thought. "He will not be able to resist the
offer I am going to make to him tonight."

Huémac tossed his head, laughed and drank. He
turned at a slight sound and in front of him stood a
young man dressed in a white cotton gown. An aura
of light surrounded the man. Huémac instinctively
reached for his weapon. He had not heard the man
approach."

"Who are you?" Huémac asked.

"I am Quetzalcóatl," the man answered.

Huémac stepped forward to look closer at the priest. He saw a handsome bronzed face with the high cheekbones of the Indian. The face was smooth and open, revealing a kind and open heart and the spirit and honest personality so prized by the Toltecs. The dark eyes looked intently at Huémac, and they were as direct and open as they were calm and serene.

If the soul truly is revealed in the face and bearing of man, Huémac thought, then this man is a god. He was impressed by the priest who stood in front of him, and he felt energy and power radiate from Quetzalcóatl. Quetzalcóatl's long, dark hair fell to his shoulders. He was not dressed in the ornate costumes with which the priests of Tezcatlipoca and Huitzilopochtli draped themselves. His gown was white cotton embroidered with green quetzal feathers, the mark of nobility. This is a handsome young priest of the Sun, a man who radiates with an aura of power, Huémac admitted to himself.

"Quetzalcóatl," Huémac said, repeating the name.

"*Quetzal*," Quetzalcóatl said, "the sacred bird of our people, feathers of the wind, wings which rise to greet the Sun, our Father. *Coatl*, the serpent, creature of the earth our mother. From these two words comes my name, I am the Plumed Serpent." ♥ Jesus

"The Plumed Serpent," Huémac whispered. Quetzacóatl, he remembered, one of the four sons of Ometéotl. Who was this man he was facing, Huémac pondered, was he only a man, a priest, or. . . .

35

"I am a priest of the House of the Dawn," Quetzalcóatl said softly.

Huémac shook his head. He stepped back to break the intensity of Quetzalcóatl's gaze. God or sorcerer, Huémac thought, I must be careful. This man is full of a strange power.

"You sent for me," Quetzalcóatl said.

"Yes," Huémac nodded and motioned for Quetzalcóatl to take a seat.

The priest sat, and Huémac, to quiet the trembling he felt in his hands and knees poured a fresh cup of pulque and drank. He poured another cup for Quetzalcóatl and offered it to the priest.

"I offer you a drink of pulque," Huémac said. He held out the bowl.

Quetzalcóatl held up his hand. "As a priest of the Sun I cannot drink that which takes away my senses."

Huémac looked at the young priest and frowned. Surely Quetzalcóatl knew it was an insult to refuse the host's drink. Then he shrugged and thought, no matter, I did not call the priest here as a drinking companion.

"Who am I?" Huémac asked.

Quetzalcóatl nodded. "You are Huémac, Lord of Tollán, warrior of the Toltecs."

So, Huémac thought, the young priest did not quake in the presence of Huémac, perhaps that was just as well. Huémac was tired of the sycophants who daily came to grovel at his feet, sputtering titles to please him. He sat, sipped his pulque and gazed at the young priest. He must go slowly, then propose the alliance.

"You call yourself a priest of the Sun, and yet I hear you do not perform sacrifices to the Sun. You call yourself a priest, and yet you do not drink the drink of the gods. I am interested in your story," Huémac said.

They faced each other, the ruler of Tollán and the priest Quetzalcóatl. One, devoted to the material world, the other, devoted to poetry and song and the spiritual teachings of the Ancient Word. Sitting across from each other they were a study in contrasts.

"I will tell my story if it pleases Lord Huémac," Quetzalcóatl responded. Huémac nodded. In the cool of the fragrant garden, in the evening light, Quetzalcóatl began his story.

"As you know, Lord Huémac, four times our Father Sun has been created, and four times his span of time has ended and he has died. It was during the last time of darkness that the gods assembled to restore life to the Sun: Who shall live on earth? the gods asked. Who shall praise the gods and perform the ceremonies of the Sun? These are the questions the gods asked as they assembled in the womb of night. They praised Ometéotl, our Lord and Lady of Duality. Ometéotl, he who is both Father and Mother, male and female, he is the foundation of the universe. Long ago, Ometéotl the Giver of Life begat four sons. One was the red Tezcatlipoca, one was the black Tezcatlipoca of authority and power, the third was given the name Quetzalcóatl. . . . "

Lord Huémac leaned forward listening intently as he heard these words, but he did not interrupt. He knew the story of creation, but it had been many years since his instruction in these ancient teachings.

"The fourth and smallest is the God of War, the god the wandering Aztecs call Huitzilopochtli, the left-handed hummingbird. These four gods are the four forces which activate the evolution and development of the world. These are the sons of Ometéotl, our Lord Who is Everywhere."

Quetzalcóatl paused. He waited for a response from Lord Huémac, but Huémac said nothing.

"Six hundred years have passed since the birth of the four brother gods," Quetzalcóatl continued. "The four gods came together to establish the laws of the universe. The gods agreed that Quetzalcóatl and Huitzilopochtli would create the world. First these gods of power created fire and the half-sun which gave little light. Then they created man and woman and sent them to cultivate the earth. They commanded the woman to spin and weave and to give birth to the people of the earth. The gods gave the woman grains of corn for making cures and soothsaying and witchcraft. Then the gods made the days and months. They gave each month twenty days, and they created eighteen months.

"Next the Lord and Lady of Mictlan were created, and they were assigned the realm of Mictlan, which is the realm of the underworld. Thus did the Lord and Lady of the Dead come into being.

"Then the gods created the heavens, to the thirteenth level, and they created the waters. And from the waters they created an enormous fish, a fish like a Golden Carp, and from this fish the earth was made.

"But these four gods, these elements of earth, air, fire and water, these four cosmic quarters of the universe were forever in battle. Each one fought for supremacy of the universe. Quetzalcóatl fought the three Tezcatlipocas, one of which was Huitzilopochtli. As each god ascended, a new age was born.

"The first Sun had its beginning 2,513 years ago. That Sun was named Four-Tiger and it lasted 676 years. The people ate acorns, and in the year One-Reed they were eaten by ocelots and the Sun was destroyed. Then came the end of the first age of man and woman.

"The second Sun was called Four-Wind, and it lasted 364 years. Quetzalcóatl was the Sun. The people ate a grain which grew in the water. Then Tezcatlipoca battled Quetzalcóatl, and a great wind arose and destroyed everything. The people became monkeys. And so the age of the Second Sun ended.

"Four-Rain was the third Sun. The people lived under this Sun 312 years, but then everything was consumed by fire and all perished. The people ate a seedlike corn, and they were like large birds, not like the humans we know today. They died in the rain of fire.

"The fourth Sun was called Four-Water, and it lasted 676 years. The people cultivated a seedlike corn, from this small grain our own corn would grow, but fifty-two years of rain came, and the people were swallowed by the waters and became fish. They perished, even the mountains disappeared under the waters.

"The fifth Sun under which we live is called Four-Movement. It is the Sun of Movement, and our people are sustained by corn. But the elders and the Ancient Word say it too will disappear, there will be earthquakes and hunger, and our end shall come. This is the Sun of the Lord Quetzalcóatl of Tollán!"

The priest's conclusion of his story was emphatic. Huémac started and leaned forward. In the dim light of the evening he was aware of a radiant light around the priest. Huémac had allowed himself to be carried away by the story of creation. Now as he looked at the priest he could tell the priest sincerely believed the story. He believed he was the god Quetzalcóatl, and spoke as if he had been at the birth and death of those four prior ages.

"Shall I continue?" Quetzalcóatl asked.

"Continue," Huémac assented.

"With the approach of the fifth age in the history of the world the gods met and pondered how to rescue the Sun from the western darkness where it lay imprisoned. And so, in the womb of night the gods spoke. The god Skirt of Stars and Light of Day spoke in the dark and empty silence. The Lord of the Waters and He Who Comes in Place of Others spoke. In the darkness, even He Who Makes the Earth Firm spoke. And I, Quetzalcóatl, god of art and wisdom and teacher of farmers, I, too, spoke." ✔ Jesus ?

Huémac shuddered when he heard these words. Had he heard correctly? The young priest of the radiant light, this man sitting across from him in his garden had called himself the deity Quetzalcóatl. It was one thing for a priest to take the honorary title of Quetzalcóatl, but this young man spoke in the first person. He actually called himself Quetzalcóatl, the god.

Huémac put aside his bowl of pulque and listened carefully. Either he was in the presence of a madman who considered himself a god, or he was in the presence of someone who had a great revelation to offer.

"Then I spoke to the gods," Quetzalcóatl continued. "I told them that I would go to the Land of the Dead to bring back the bones of man and woman. So I traveled to Mictlan to retrieve the bones of mankind. When I arrived in Mictlan I claimed the precious bones of mankind from the Lord and Lady of Mictlan. Like the planet Venus I circled beneath the earth to the dark land. There I blew into my trumpet shell, and my breath was the spirit of life for the precious bones. Four times I circled the golden realm. From the east I came, then from the south and west and north. Like the four seasons which bring their fruit then die to renew again, I came. As Quetzalcóatl, the writhing serpent of wind, I came. As the breath of life, I came.

"I will take the precious bones of man and woman

with me," I said, but the Lord of the Dead tricked me and made me sleep. Then came the birds of Mictlan, the crowned quail, they nibbled the precious bones, and in so doing afflicted mankind with mortality. A part of mankind belonged forever more to the dead, the fleshless ones. When I awoke, I wept. Man and woman now owed a time of return to the Land of the Dead.

"Then my soul spoke to me. Do not weep, Quetzalcóatl. Man is mortal, but in song and poetry and art he can be immortal. This you will teach mankind.

"So I gathered the precious bones in a bundle and delivered them to Quilaztli, she who is Serpent Woman, our Earth Mother. She gound the bones into powder and placed them in a jadestone bowl. With a jade knife I then pierced my flesh so that my blood was mixed in with the precious bones.

"So it was that Earth Mother and I gave birth to man and woman, the servants of the gods.

"But man must eat," the gods said to me.

"Then I, Quetzalcóatl, changed myself into a black ant and I followed the red ant into the Mountain of Food. From there I brought kernels of maize, the corn for man to plant and eat. The gods chewed the kernels of maize and laid the food at the lips of man, First Man and First Woman, they who were named Oxomoco and Cipactónal. ♥ Adam & Eve

"I will bring the Mountain of Food to you, I told First Man and First Woman, but I could not move the mountain. First Man and First Woman cast ker-

nels of corn and divined that it was Nanahuatl, the
God of Lightning Who Is Covered With Sores, who
should break open the mountain. Nanahuatl did
break open the mountain, but as he was old and fee-
ble and covered with sores he fell asleep; then the
rain gods came and stole the corn. From the four sacred directions they came: the blue, white, yellow
and red rain gods. All of the foods were stolen by
these gods and delivered to mankind."

Here the priest Quetzalcóatl paused in his story.
Lord Huémac sighed, a deep, disturbing sigh. He remembered the story of creation. He was tempted to
believe the priest. The gods had revealed the Ancient
Word to man; now the Toltecs were the mightiest
empire in all of Mexico. Perhaps the gods had sent a
new teacher to Tollán. What a rare opportunity that
would be for Huémac if he used it to his advantage.
After all, no other nation could lay claim to such a
wise man. Imagine the power of an alliance between
himself and Quetzalcóatl? Tollán would become the
center of the earth. He would raise armies to conquer the earth, and Quetzalcóatl would continue to
disperse his knowledge of art and agriculture. As
long as Quetzalcóatl did not interfere in the politics
of the empire and in the business of war, Huémac
felt he could be controlled. What a powerful alliance
it would be!

Lord Huémac smiled. Destiny had brought together the ruler of Tollán and the priest.

"Your story is one of divine mystery," Huémac

43

said. "You have been the instigator of marvelous accomplishments in our city, but I sense a greater destiny awaiting us!"

"Yes," Quetzalcóatl replied. "I have much work left to do."

Huémac was not listening. He was only hearing his own internal voice which spoke of his personal greatness.

"Tollán will be an imperial city!" Huémac said with excitement.

"Tollán will be great," Quetzalcóatl repeated, but his voice was tinged with sadness. He had seen into the stream of time, and he knew what lay ahead.

"So we will make a pact!" Huémac said and rose. "Together we will build a grand city, Tollán of the western sun!"

He raised his bowl of pulque, and in his excitement he spilled the liquid. He drank, toasted his luck, then looked at the priest who sat quietly watching him.

"Agreed," Huémac said.

Quetzalcóatl rose and looked at Huémac. In the dark of the garden Quetzalcóatl's aura was a golden light which outshone the stars in the sky.

"I cannot make such a pact with any earthly ruler," Quetzalcóatl said.

"But why?" the incredulous Huémac demanded.

"I have come to teach the way of light and wisdom," Quetzalcóatl answered, "Mine is not the way of war."

"Then you are a fool!" Huémac sputtered.

"I offer you an alliance of grandeur! I offer you riches! The Toltec Empire will spread from sea to sea! And you will be the chief priest of my empire."

Quetzalcóatl reached out and touched Huémac, and Huémac trembled at the power he felt in the touch of the priest.

"You must listen to me," Quetzalcóatl said. "You must listen to my story. My destiny is to make Tollán great, but it must be through the study of art and wisdom. I will come again and reveal the rest of my story."

Then he was gone, leaving the trembling Huémac alone in the dark garden.

Three

*T*he following day Lord Huémac anxiously awaited the arrival of Quetzalcóatl. He was in an uneasy mood. His informants all said the same thing: the priest Quetzalcóatl had a great following, they called him Topiltzin, Our Dear Prince. Prince? The Toltecs had Lord Huémac, that was enough. The title was not an earthly title, the informants said, for Quetzalcóatl was not interested in earthly rule. He is a teacher, they said, teaching the wisdom of the Ancient Word, art, knowledge, and the science of raising crops.

I have been blind, Huémac thought to himself. I have not been aware of the works of this priest, and the spread of his influencce. Has Tlacahuepan kept this knowledge from me? It was clear from the informants that Tlacahuepan and the other high priests of Tezcatlipoca were jealous of Quetzalcóatl.

I have been too engrossed in the wars, Huémac thought. The warriors are the might and power of the Toltec Empire. Without them to guard the borders of our beloved Tollán, all would be lost. All art and knowledge would crumble away under the invasions by other tribes. It is the warriors who kept the society of the Toltecs safe. Without us there would be nothing.

But now there are two great men in Tollán, Quetzalcóatl and myself. We are opposites, but still there is the possibility we can work together. But he must come under my rule, he must be my chief priest. He must bend his will to mine.

Huémac reached for his bowl of pulque, plucked a flower from a hanging vine and thought of Butterfly Woman. He had been to the baths that afternoon and the touch of her hands and her fragrance still lingered on his body. His problems seemed to disappear when he sought his pleasure with her. Huémac smiled as he recalled the hours spent with Butterfly Woman, but even as he recalled his mistress, he felt a presence behind him. He turned to see the high priest Quetzalcóatl.

"Good evening, Lord Huémac," Quetzalcóatl said. Perfectly composed, glowing with radiant light, he was an image of beauty.

"Come forward, priest," Huémac commanded, disturbed at the way the priest seemed to appear from nowhere. "Do you always enter unannounced?"

"But I am announced," Quetzalcóatl smiled. "Every morning as the morning star rises in the House Made of Dawn to prepare the way for our Father the Sun, I am announced."

"You speak in metaphor," Huémac answered.

"I speak directly and honestly to you, Lord Huémac."

"Then am I to believe you are the morning star," Huémac smiled.

"Believe what the gods reveal to your heart," Quetzalcóatl answered.

"Am I to believe your story?" Huémac asked.

"As you will," Quetzalcóatl answered, and again he refused the offer of pulque. "Destiny has brought us to Tollán, and we cannot escape our destiny."

Huémac nodded. There was an appealing presence to the young priest, in spite of his arrogance. How did he come to be as he was?

"You did not finish your story yesterday evening. Will you please continue."

Quetzalcóatl began. "I was born in the year Ce Acatl, One Reed, the day the morning star appeared in the heavens. I was reared by Quilaztli, Serpent Woman. Four days my mother suffered with my birth and on the fourth day she died. My father is the Sun, and as a young man I proved myself as a warrior at my father's side."

How interesting, Huémac thought, the young man was once a warrior. He did not understand that Quetzalcóatl was speaking of a cosmic struggle which had to do with the gods and the planets and stars of the heavens.

"My uncles, the four hundred Mimixoca, the innumerable stars of the sky, hated my father and killed him; they buried him beneath the western mountains. The day they killed him, night fell, and so I

went looking for my Father, the Sun, asking everywhere: Where is my father? A vulture told me they
had buried my father's body beneath the western
mountains. I retrieved the corpse of my father and
placed it within the temple which is called Cloud Serpent Mountain. Yes, just as kings are buried in the
pyramid temples, I placed my father in his temple.

"Then the moles helped me dig a passage through
the temple, and I ascended and lit the fire of the
dawn. My father had died and an age had come to
an end, but I rekindled the fire. The eagle, jaguar and
wolf were there to help me.

"My uncles became very angry. They wanted to
control the light at the top of the temple, and they
attempted to climb to the top, but I struck them and
sent them tumbling down. I put my uncles to their
death. The animals watched as I conquered my uncles. The brave animals helped as I slew my father's.
brothers."

Huémac shivered as he heard this gruesome tale.
The priest spoke fervently, with excitement. Yes, he
had murdered his uncles and paved the way for his
father. He had been a warrior in his early days. That
is good, Huémac thought, he has a taste for war.

"Then I journeyed to the east," Quetzalcóatl continued. He was inspired as he told his story, his presence was a burning torch in the dark garden. "I went
to the Divine Waters of the East."

Here Quetzalcóatl paused and sighed. Time was a
cycle of death and renewal. He peered into time and
saw his own death. His death and his legend would

pass on in story through the centuries. The future would know the story of the Lord of the Dawn, the Plumed Serpent who made Tollán great. The story would never die, but he and Tollán would die, they would be swept into the great stream of time which circled the universe.

He looked at Lord Huémac, and he knew he could not reveal that on the eastern waters Quetzalcóatl would die. There he would be cremated and consumed by the flames. In the House of the Dawn he would rise as the morning star.

"Go on," Huémac said. He felt agitated by the story, but he wanted to hear the conclusion.

"I prepared a path for my Father the Sun," Quetzalcóatl said. "He is the Fifth Sun, the Sun of Movement. He has come to rule over this new age. . . . "

"No!" Huémac shouted and jumped to his feet. He was suddenly conscious of the true impact of Quetzalcoatl's words. "What you say cannot be true! You place yourself in the realm of the gods! You call the Sun your father and the stars your uncles. Don't you see the blasphemy! For your words you can be punished."

"I shall be punished," Quetzalcóatl said softly.

"Renounce what you say!" Huémac insisted. "Repeat it no more. This claim you make to be of the realm of the gods can only bring you grief. You have helped the people of Tollán, you have respect and esteem, but you must renounce this claim of deity!"

"I cannot renounce my nature," Quetzalcóatl answered.

"Then you are a fool and will be cursed," Huémac cried. He was angry. But the priest was no fool, he was calm, composed. Still, Huémac needed the priest and his followers. He had to be careful.

"Listen, priest. For your words I could banish you. As lightning splits the tree, I could destroy you. But I don't want to kill you, I want to join with you to make our Toltec nation the greatest ever seen. You have many followers, let us join forces, forget this nonsense of the gods, and you will become rich and powerful. Join me, become my high priest and all of Tula will come to pray at your temple." Temptation

Huémac waited breathlessly. Ah, if only Quetzal-cóatl would say yes, together they could create a kingdom which would last forever. The Toltec Empire would spread from sea to sea.

"I cannot accept your offer," Quetzalcóatl answered. "I have my work to do. . . ." Jesus

"You cannot accept my offer!" Huémac sputtered. "Don't you realize I am offering you a share in the Toltec Empire? What manner of man are you? I offer to take you into my counsel, into my family, and you refuse. . . ."

Huémac paused. His family? Yes, to draw the power and the followers of Quetzalcóatl into his fold he would take the priest into his family. That was the thing to do! The priest could not refuse his daughter. She was the most beautiful virgin in all of Tollán. Many suitors had come to ask for her in marriage, noblemen with great wealth, captains who commanded many warriors, and other princes from the provinces. In this past year as she became a woman Huémac had guarded Precious Gem. No man would have her. He had decided her beauty was for himself alone.

But Quetzalcóatl had many followers. Huémac commanded the warriors, and the Jaguar and the Eagle Cults ruled, but the Toltecs long ago had decreed that there should be a balance in the society, and that harmony should be kept so all quarters had an equal voice. Now, by joining Quetzalcóatl's strength to his own, Huémac saw the obvious way to dominate the two large factions of Tollán. It was a stroke of luck the gods had cast into his destiny. He must use it, and the way to accomplish his goal was to use his daughter. He shuddered at the thought of giving away his Precious Gem, but he was cunning enough to see the necessity of it.

With the priest married into his family, Quetzalcóatl's followers would fall in line. That was the way of the Toltecs, that the son-in-law would be obedient to the father. And after all, his daughter would still be at home, she would be married but she would still live in the palace of Huémac. Her beauty would still fill his days.

"Listen," Huémac said calmly. "I understand why you would not want to make this association. You are a priest, I am the Lord of Tollán, but we are not that different. Together we could unite Tollán, but I respect your wish, and I ask forgiveness for my outburst. I know in my heart that if we brought our forces together Tollán would be the greatest of all cities."

"I cannot serve two masters," Quetzalcóatl answered. "My work is to spread the light of my Father, the Sun, so that the people may know his divine power. I am a bringer of poetry, art and knowledge. That is the path to the eternal truth. . . . the only path," he added.

Huémac held his temper in check. The young priest was fixed in his way. But Huémac knew men and the strong instincts which fed the fire of desire. He knew how men could fall from greatness. He knew the beauty of his daughter. Let Quetzalcóatl see her in all her beauty, he thought, and his path to eternal truth will take a turn. The beauty of women was a truth he knew. He smiled.

"Let us continue our discussion," Huémac said. "Come to my garden in two nights, when the moon is full. I have something to offer you. Will you come?"

Quetzacóatl nodded. He understood the temptation clothed in Huémac's words, but he also knew he would be tempted many times while he lived in the body of a man. He could not hide from temptations, he had to encounter and overcome each one. This was the way to understand the heart of man. He had come to Tollán to understand the flesh, to understand why man had left the teachings of the Ancient Word. He knew the path he followed in the heavens, far away from the realm of man. Now he had to understand that other side of his nature, that heart of man which throbbed within his chest.

As Huémac was a man of the flesh, of the earth, a reflection of the material world, so Quetzalcóatl was a reflection of the light of the spirit. Quetzalcóatl knew that long after his destiny was completed, all of mankind would come to understand this. So he accepted Huémac's invitation.

"I will come when the moon is full," Quetzalcóatl answered.

Four

uémac spent the rest of the night in restless
contemplation. On the one hand, he was
pleased that he was about to ensnare Quetzalcóatl, and that the priest would soon be under his
control. But on the other hand he would be losing
his daughter, his greatest source of joy in the palace.
Like other Toltec nobles, Huémac followed the prac-
tice of keeping his daughter secluded at home. The
Ancient Word preached against the custom, but this
transgression and others had crept into the life-style
of the indolent noble class.

In the morning Huémac went to his daughter's
quarters. He paused near a curtained door so he
could watch without being observed. Precious Gem
was bathing. She stood on a reed mat while her
maids gathered about her. Huémac could hear their
laughter and chatter. Like a flower bathed in dew,
Precious Gem stood on the mat, her bronze body
glistening with water. She sang as the maids put
aside the clay pots and began to dry her, caressing
her soft skin with fragrant oils. One maid began to

braid her hair, a second covered the body of her mistress with a simple cotton gown.

She is indeed a goddess, Huémac thought. Even the maids who waited on her considered her a goddess, her beauty was so perfect. In the way of the Toltec the more perfectly formed the body, the truer the character and the soul. To them, Precious Gem was a woman who would give birth to gods. Now that she had reached womanhood, she was ready to marry.

Huémac called, announcing himself. The maids scurried away. Precious Gem came to him.

"I have come to tell you that tomorrow evening when the moon is full you are to be in the garden. You are to dress as befits a princess who is ready for marriage," Huémac said. He spoke slowly, so his voice would not betray his feelings.

"Marry?" Precious Gem asked. "To whom shall I be married?"

"The priest Quetzalcóatl," Huémac replied. Then he turned and quickly walked away, leaving his daughter stunned by surprise.

She had once seen the young priest as he spoke in the marketplace. He was handsome beyond all men; all of the young women commented on this. Would he take a wife, they asked each other, or would he remain wedded to his work and vision? Precious Gem now realized that her father had made an arrangement with the young priest. Excitement coursed through her body as she ran to discuss the plan with her mother.

Time was short—for the remaining two days and into the night preparations were made. A new gown of quetzal feathers was woven; jewels were chosen, each piece of gold ornamented with precious stones sparkled with light. Perfumes made from crushed flowers were sprinkled in her bath. Her face shone with the glow befitting a virgin bride.

On the appointed evening Precious Gem, arrayed in her finery, looked like a goddess. The maids bowed and stepped back as their young mistress came forth. They had never seen her so beautiful.

Already the servants had whispered the news beyond the walls of Huémac's home. The city of the Toltecs buzzed with excitement. Would the priest Quetzalcóatl marry the daughter of Huémac?

It seemed everyone was pleased. The nobles knew the young priest would temper Huémac's militaristic nature. The merchants yearned for peace since the war was good only for those who traded in supplies for war. Mothers yearned for their sons to return home and satisfy their manliness by playing in the ball games instead of making war. Even the priests and the wise men, while they debated the subject of married priests, had to admit that this would certainly help turn the society and its leader away from the costly wars of the past year. Who knew? Perhaps it was in the destiny of the priest Quetzalcóatl to change the nature even of Huémac, to turn the entire society toward a new path, a new greatness. Everyone prayed to Omotéotl, the Lord of the Close Vicinity.

Precious Gem stepped into the main room of the palace. The room was aglow and sparkling with the light of torches and candles. Lord Huémac, dressed in his most elegant costume, waited. Lady Huémac, also elegant in her gown of quetzal and cotton, went to her daughter and embraced her.

"Now you will become a wife, a mother," she whispered. She wanted to say more, but she knew her time would come. Now it was time for the father to address the daughter, using the words prescribed by custom. She stood by her daughter and Huémac stepped forward to speak.

"Listen to me, my Precious Gem," Huémac began. "I want you to understand that you are of a noble line. You are now a lady, a precious gem. You are a turquoise. As a flower, you are the offshoot and the stem. My blood is in you, you are a descendant of noble lineage. As long as you live on earth, remain a lady, remain my Precious Gem.

"Now that you are to marry I must tell you how life is: On this earth there is no happiness, no pleasure. There is only heartache, worry and fatigue. This is the earth of suffering and distress. On this earth there are tears and crying, our bodies grow old and our strength is worn out by bitterness and discouragement. The wind blows cold and sharp as obsidian. The sun burns us and we perish of thirst and hunger. That is the way it is on this earth.

"Listen, my Precious Gem, there is no well-being on this earth, there is no happiness, there is no pleasure. The elders say the earth is a place of painful pleasure, of grievous happiness. The elders also say that we should not moan our situation, we should not be filled with sadness. The Lord of Near and Far, Ometéotl, has given us laughter, sleep, food; he has given us strength and fortitude and the act by which you will bring children into the world. All this sweetens life on earth. This is the way life is on earth. Will you be fearful? Will you weep?

"No. Because you are of the nobility, there is authority on earth. Do not think of putting an end to your life. Do not cry. Be noble, like a warrior of the Jaguar Cult. Struggle and work. You are of a renowned family, you are born from illustrious people. Awaken early, arise with the dawn. Invoke Him, the Lord, our Lord Ometéotl. He who is the Lord of Everywhere will hear you and look upon you with compassion. He will grant you your destiny, that path which is set aside for you. Guard your destiny, that portion of life which came with you at birth, and if it be bad, pray to the Lord that he change it.

"Rise early, wash your hands and feet, cleanse your mouth, go forth and sweep your home and hearth. Do not be idle. Prepare the fire, stay close to the fire, burn copal. Prepare food and drink for your family, spin and weave, fulfill your womanly duties. Learn to embroider as a Toltec daughter, prepare and dye the cotton. Do not be idle, be strict with yourself. Remember the history of our lords, our ancient heritage.

"Watch who would be your enemy. Make yourself strong so you may be proud to be a Toltec woman.

Remember my words: Watch who would be your enemy. And remember, your father is your lord above all others."

These were the words of Huémac, the words prescribed by custom. He said them forcefully, as was the custom, and yet in his heart he was sad. His beautiful daughter, she who stood obediently before him, she who was truly a precious gem, would be leaving his side. Because he yearned to fulfill his own destiny and be the greatest ruler in all of the history of Tollán, he would give her away. He truly believed his destiny was the destiny of Tollán.

Now it was time for the mother to step forward and speak:

"My precious dove, my little daughter, my girl. Now the time has come for you to leave our side. Listen well to your father's words, for he is of noble line. As you are his blood, you are my blood and my color. As he gave you advice on all matters, I too must speak my heart to you. I must fulfill my duty. Keep our words as precious stones, like fine turquoise, treasure our words like a painting in your heart. Educate your sons and make them men, and pass on to them what we say.

"I am your mother, I carried you near my bosom, and when you were born I lulled you to sleep. I placed you in your cradle every night, I held you in my arms, my milk nourished you.

"Listen, you must follow the way of our wise and ancient ladies. They left us their wisdom, and this is what they said: Our life on earth is difficult. We wander as if lost, and on one side there is an abyss, on the other a ravine. To keep her virtue a woman must walk only in the middle. Remember this, my dove, my daughter. A woman does not deliver her body foolishly. If you do, you will be full of misery and anguish. Give yourself only to your husband, and allow no other man to use you. Do not deceive your husband. If you are wanton, you will give a bad name to your ancestors, you will cast dung on their history. Then your husband will cast you out in the street and you will be dragged about. The people will crush your skull, they will destroy you.

"Be an exemplary woman so that the people will not gossip about you. If you commit sexual transgressions the Lord of the Close Vicinity, He Who is Near and Far, will be angered. Then truly our Lord Who is Near and Far will send you paralysis or blindness. Then you will be in tatters, in rags, you will be despised by your man. Then Ometéotl, the Lord Who is Everywhere, will trample you and send you to Our Common House, the Place of the Dead.

"The Master, Our Lord, is also merciful. But if you behave improperly and betray your husband, you will not live in peace. Time on earth is brief. Be virtuous. Do not bring shame on your forefathers and their name. Bring us honor. Be happy my precious dove. Always walk with Ometéotl, the Lord of the Near and Far."

This is what Lady Huémac said to her daughter, then she took her hand and they followed Lord Huémac into the portico and out into the garden. It was a still night. The full moon shone brightly, creating a silver sheen on the grass and the green leaves. It was a night of splendor, with the fragrance of jasmine and jacaranda in the air. There in the middle of the garden the young priest waited, and he too looked like a god in his raiment of white cotton and quetzal feathers.

Precious Gem felt her pulse quicken when she saw Quetzalcóatl. He was truly a handsome man. As was proper, Precious Gem looked down as she approached the priest, but her heart throbbed with anticipation. What would he say? Would he open his heart to her?

Quetzalcóatl saw Huémac approach, and when he saw Lady Huémac with her daughter dressed in the raiment of a princess, he fully understood the significance of Huémac's invitation, he would be offered the daughter as a wife. Now he knew how much Huémac would offer for the alliance with the priest of the Ancient Word.

Huémac stopped. He turned and looked at his wife as she led Precious Gem forward. The young woman stood directly in front of Quetzalcóatl. "I offer you my daughter, my blood, my family," Huémac said. That was all he needed to say.

In the portico where the maids and servants waited breathlessly, there was a murmur. Instantly the message was whispered and carried out into the streets where the people of the city waited. Huémac had offered his daughter to Quetzelcóatl. The people waited in silence. Would Quetzalcóatl accept her?

On the portico, well out of sight of everyone, only Tlacahuepan frowned. Curse Huémac, and curse his daughter, and curse this union, he thought, and he prayed for chaos and disruption. He prayed to Tezcatlipoca, the god of darkness, to come and interfere with the proposed union. Tezcatlipoca heard him, and a whirlwind filled the courtyard. The flames of the torches sputtered and went out. The servants felt the quick, powerful wind and were afraid. They felt the presence of the dark god interfering with the proposed marriage.

Quetzalcóatl felt it too, but he paid no attention to the turbulent wind which could not move him. He knew the ways of Tezcatlipoca, and he did not fear him. He raised his hand and the wind grew quiet. Then he looked at the girl in front of him. He had never seen a more beautiful woman. Her oval face, her arched eyebrows, her clear dark eyes. Her slender neck curved down to smooth, round shoulders. He sensed the tremor in her breast as she looked up and gazed into his eyes. Both felt immediate love in their gaze.

Precious Gem shivered, although the night was not cool. In the full moonlight she felt for the first time like a woman. A yearning, a tremble, passed through her heart, gathered like butterflies in her stomach, made her heart pound, made her legs tremble. She had seen the aura which surrounded Quetzalcóatl; now she saw the same light in his eyes. The light of infinity floated as a serene message of love in his clear eyes.

Quetzalcóatl also felt love, he sensed the tremble of her body and he felt his response to the young woman. Yes, she was a precious gem, she would give birth to gods. For a moment the young priest felt confused. He had many sisters whom he loved, but he had never felt love in this way. This was the love of a woman that a man feels stirring in his blood. He had loved the Toltecs and for that love he had brought them his arts and the wisdom of the ages. He had become a man, as one of them, and now he had to act and choose as one of them.

"You honor me with your beauty," Quetzalcóatl whispered to Precious Gem. She smiled. She was pleasing in his eyesight, and that made her happy. He took her hand and his touch relieved her tension, but she said nothing. The decision was his. She was ready to go with him at a moment's notice, her heart had spoken to her as she gazed into his eyes, and she knew she would always be obedient to him.

Quetzalcóatl turned and looked at Huémac. "You do me an honor, for you offer me the wealth of Tollán."

Huémac smiled, put his hands on his sides and rocked on his heels. He had predicted the outcome, he knew the power of his daughter's beauty. A priest can marry and still continue his duties, Huémac thought, and our searcher after the eternal truth, our celibate young priest is about to answer the call of the blood.

"You are indeed a precious gem," Quetzalcóatl said to the girl. "The most precious flower in

Tollán." He reached out and touched her cheek. It was hot to his touch. His touch sent a warm flush through her body. Has he accepted me? she thought.

Lord Huémac smiled, his wife smiled. They had seen the priest touch their daughter, they saw how fondly he looked on her. They saw their daughter close her eyes to his touch, they saw the glow on her lovely face. Love had come to the bargain.

"But the high priest of the Sun cannot take a wife," Quetzalcóatl whispered. The girl opened her eyes. She looked into his eyes, and now she saw something new in his eyes. Yes, love was still there, but it was not the carnal love of passion, it was another kind of love. In his eyes shone the bright light of the moon, the stars of the firmament. His love was from another world. It was the love he bore for all of the Toltecs, he had come to raise them to a height of unsurpassed civilization. His destiny was in the hands of Ometéotl.

"The Ancient Word forbids me—" Quetzalcóatl said, and Precious Gem nodded. She understood. He had not refused her; he had simply chosen to continue his destiny without a wife, without children, without home. That was the way of the priests of the Morning Star, the Plumed Serpent which rose before the Father Sun in the House Made of Dawn.

"I understand your wishes," she replied, then as gracefully as her trembling legs could carry her she turned and walked to her mother's side. Now the stunned Huémac thundered with fury. He had heard the words of refusal, he had seen his daughter put aside, returned to her mother as a common man would put aside bad pumpkins at the marketplace.

"The Ancient Word!" Huémac shouted. "This is no time to consider the Ancient Word! You are a man! I have offered you my daughter! Do you dare to refuse my offer!" He stepped forward, his neck and shoulders and arms bulging with fury. From a nearby bench he grabbed his war club.

"My Lord!" Lady Huémac called and rushed forward. "He is a priest of the Sun! We must accept his decision! He cannot be harmed!" She had been afraid of this, she had known it was possible for the priest to refuse an offer of marriage because of his role in Toltec society. She threw her arms around Lord Huémac to stop him. Huémac shook her off and sent her reeling, then he raised his club to strike Quetzalcóatl.

"No!" Huémac's daughter cried. She threw her arms around Quetzalcóatl, ready to receive the first blow. "Do not strike him, father," she pleaded. "I accept his decision. His vow does not allow him to marry."

She sobbed as she held the young priest tightly, protecting him as best she could. She had been refused and for a moment she had felt shamed. But she had looked into his eyes and she understood why he could not take a wife. His destiny was clear in his eyes. He was a god from the heavens; his destiny was to make the Toltecs great.

"I accept his decision," she repeated and looked at

her father. Huémac stood with outstretched arm, club poised to strike. His body shuddered with anger, his temples throbbed with the shame he felt. The young priest had dishonored him by refusing his daughter. If it were not for his daughter clinging to the priest and covering him with her body he would crush his skull with one blow, he would feed the carcass to the dogs in the marketplace and dare the heavens to punish him for the murder of this priest.

Everyone waited with bated breath. Lady Huémac on the ground where she fell could only pray, the servants in the shadows of the portico, mouths open, waited for the blow to fall. Tlacahuepan, a broad grin on his face, prayed for the murder of Quetzalcóatl. But slowly Huémac's arm came down, he cast aside the war club.

"I have offered you my most valuable treasure," Huémac said, "and by refusing her you shame me. The people of Tollán will say I have no honor." He struggled to control the violence he felt in his blood. Now his voice became hard and cutting. "Listen, priest, you have had your chance. Now I say to you, I will not kill you tonight, but I swear by the god Tezcatlipoca, I will destroy you. I will look only for the day when you are brought down and made utterly despicable. You will lose everything—your arts, your culture, and your followers. You will be made to grovel in the slime. This I promise you!" Huémac turned and marched from his garden, calling for his Captain as he went. He needed a drink of pulque, he needed to wash away all the bitterness he felt in his blood. Lady Huémac rose and took her trembling daughter in her arms and turned to Quetzalcóatl.

"You must leave," Lady Huémac said. "It is dangerous for you here."

Quetzalcóatl bowed. He knew the girl understood, and that was enough. He turned and left the garden, leaving Lady Huémac and Precious Gem.

Five

Now the stage for conflict between Huémac, the earthly ruler, and Quetzalcóatl, the priest of the Sun, was set. In the marketplace the people told and retold the story. The wise men and the followers of Quetzalcóatl defended the young priest, declaring he had acted properly. The Ancient Word forbade the marriage of the priest. It would be wrong for the young priest to make an alliance with Huémac, a man who only knew the ways of war. Quetzalcóatl, they argued, had done what he must do; now he could continue his work for the Toltecs without being encumbered by Huémac's rule.

Most of the people of Tollán agreed, but some were sad because they thought that Quetzalcóatl in the household of Huémac would have been a modifying influence on the strict ruler. Even as they spoke Huémac unleashed his full fury and made wars on his neighbors on all sides. Higher taxes were collected from the people to support the wars. The Captains of the Jaguar Cult were happy. With the talk of an alliance with the followers of Quetzalcóatl out of the way, they pursued their path of war and aggression. The vendors who profited from the wars also supported Huémac, they were happy for the commerce which fattened their purses.

Quetzalcóatl paid no attention to the rancor he had brought upon himself. He cast himself into his work, teaching people, encouraging participation in the arts and the pursuit of knowledge. He spoke in the city and in the countryside, and everywhere great crowds gathered to hear the man of peace, the priest some already called the Plumed Serpent. He taught art and wisdom, but he also spoke against the way of war. For this he continued to draw the wrath of Huémac.

The tlamatinime, the wise men of the Toltecs, understood the situation. In their own lifetime they had seen their civilization rise to greatness. The city grew in splendor under the guidance of Quetzalcóatl, and the wealth of conquered tribes and captives was drawn into the city by the wars of Huémac. The wise men knew that every person reflected the eternal battle of spirit and matter. The duality of forces in the universe sought reconciliation, just as the duality of forces in each person sought harmony. Spirit and matter. Had Quetzalcóatl, who was the Plumed Serpent, reconciled in his soul these two great forces? the wise men asked. And what of Huémac the materialist, the man of war, the warrior who believed only in force? Would he ever reconcile his earthly nature to the nature of spirit?

The wise men asked these questions, and they pondered them. Yes, in their own lifetime they had been privileged to see the greatness of Tollán, and they saw how greatness was the reflection of the eternal tension between spirit and matter, the sacred and the profane. Now one rose, now the other fell. Back and forth, each seeking ascendancy, as Huémac sought control over Quetzalcóatl. The two men and their destinies were microcosms of the eternal battle for equilibrium in the universe, and as the wise men reflected on this cosmic struggle, they realized the same search for harmony took place in each person. The men and women who sought spiritual understanding were drawn to Quetzalcóatl; they followed his laws and became the artisans, poets, builders and philosophers. Those drawn to the world and its material goods were drawn to Huémac, and they profited from the wars.

The wise men of the Toltecs saw this, they pondered these questions and they encouraged their students to analyze the questions of greatness and of destiny. They pointed to the young priest Quetzalcóatl and noted his work, and they pointed at Huémac and analyzed his campaigns and his philosophy. What did it mean, they asked, for a society to arrive at greatness and still be caught up in these questions? And if there was no resolution for the spirit and the material, if these two forces did not finally work in harmony, would that mark the end of the Toltec Empire? That is what the wise men feared as they discussed and analyzed the problems of their day.

Quetzalcóatl had taught the Toltecs how to plant corn, and their fields were plentiful. He had taught them to spin cotton and they put aside their skins with which they once covered themselves. He had taught them to build beautiful temples and pyramids, and his followers had built Quetzalcóatl a temple of four parts: House of Redshell, House of Whiteshell, House of Turquoise, House of Precious Feathers. When it was completed Quetzalcóatl retired to his temple to contemplate; there he, too, wrestled with the same questions which the wise men of Tollán tried to answer. It was time to retire to contemplation and think of his destiny. He had come from the house of his Father the Sun, and he had become a man, and now the desires in his blood made him question his destiny.

He prayed, then cut his flesh with sharp pieces of jadestone. There in his temple he purified his body by whipping it with fir boughs. Sometimes in his thoughts he saw Precious Gem and he felt disturbed. Her beauty still called to him, her beauty disturbed his dreams. At night, he went out to look at the heavens, to look at his sisters in the night sky, and their beauty also disturbed him. Each one called to him, as Precious Gem called to him in his dreams.

So more and more Quetzalcóatl sought refuge in his temple, he fled the temptations of desire. He sent his prayers to the Skirt of Stars and the Light of Day, he prayed to the Lord and Lady of Sustenance, he prayed to the God Clothed in Red and the God

Clothed in Black. In his prayers he called these names, the names of Ometéotl.

"Help me to help my people," Quetzalcóatl prayed. "Help me to bring them to greatness."

And Ometéotl, the Spirit of Duality, heard Quetzalcóatl and rewarded him. With his help Quetzalcóatl discovered great riches, and he taught the artisans how to use gold, silver, turquoise, jadestone, redshell and whiteshell. He taught them to weave and embroider with the plumes of the quetzal bird, the blue heron, and the spoonbill and cotinga. He taught them to plant cacao and cotton and all manner of other plants. The people of Tollán prospered. They built a huge city with many temples and wide streets and a marketplace which was the largest in all of Mexico.

News of Toltec greatness spread north to Aztlan, and south to the land of the Mayas. In the farthest regions, even in the mountains of the Andes the greatness of Tollán was known. The fame of the Toltecs spread, and from everywhere the best artisans came to learn at Tollán. The poets and philosophers came to listen to the discourse of the wise men of Tollán. Quetzalcóatl brought a golden age to Tollán, and the city became the center of civilization of Indian Mexico. This, everyone knew.

Lord Huémac saw what Quetzalcóatl built and his jealousy and hatred grew. It had begun with the refusal of his daughter by the priest, but other things fed Huémac's hate. Quetzalcóatl, as always,

preached against war and Huémac's way; also, the
young priest had become too powerful and had
many followers. Huémac secretly feared him. For
this reason Huémac plotted with his sorcerer,
Tlacahuepan, to bring about Quetzalcóatl's downfall.

"I want Quetzalcóatl out of the way!" Huémac
cried in anger. "He speaks against me, he insults the
Jaguar Cult in public, his followers refuse to pay
taxes for the wars we fight. He interferes with my
destiny to make Tollán great!"

"That is true, my Lord," Tlacahuepan answered.
"Quetzalcóatl is a thorn for all of us. Perhaps there is
a way to get rid of him . . . "

"How?" Huémac snapped.

"We must turn the force of the god Tezcatlipoca
against him. We must bargain with the God of Dark
Dreams and Confused Thoughts to give you the
strength to defeat Quetzalcóatl."

Huémac nodded. He understood what it meant to
sell one's soul to the dark god Tezcatlipoca, but to
get rid of Quetzalcóatl he would do it. To get rid of
the priest who had shamed him he would do anything.

"I will do it," Huémac said. "Tell me what I must
do."

"Sell your soul to Tezcatlipoca," Tlacahuepan
whispered. "Come and pray at his temple." Huémac
obeyed, and he prayed to the god of darkness, the
enemy of Quetzalcóatl, and even as he was praying

Tezcatlipoca plotted against Quetzalcóatl and against Huémac also, for he called no man master.

"This is what I will do," Tezcatlipoca whispered. Then he went out to impersonate a licentious Huaxtecan. The Toltecs did not like the Huaxtecans from the coast—they thought they were immoral in their actions. That is why Tezcatlipoca, impersonating a Huaxtecan, went nude into the market square that morning. With his penis dangling he went and sat at the market square to sell his chili peppers. In this way he planned to do evil.

He sat near the palace entrance and called out for all to hear: "Chili, chili! I have hot chili for sale!" He sat where he knew the daughter of Huémac would walk on her way to the market.

When Huémac's daughter approached the market square she heard the vendor calling out that he had hot chili for sale. She drew near him, and she saw his nakedness. Precious Gem became bewitched by his spell and swooned. She was carried back to her room by her maids, but it was too late; she became ill. She became swollen and inflamed, bewitched as she was by the chili vendor.

Lord Huémac was sent for and came immediately.

"What has happened?" he asked the maids. "What has happened to my daughter?"

He wept to see his beautiful daughter so swollen and pale.

"We went to the marketplace," one of the maids answered. "A Huaxtecan was selling chili peppers.

He acted in a licentious manner, he shocked Precious Gem and she fainted. That's how it happened, that's how the illness seized her." They did not dare tell him that his daughter had bought the chili of the vendor.

Lord Huémac was angry. The men from Huaxteca were his enemies. Now one had come to make his daughter ill. Perhaps the chili vendor had practiced witchcraft, perhaps he had put a curse on his daughter. Only the person who set the curse could lift the spell, so it was imperative to find the Huaxtecan and force him to cure his daughter.

"Find him!" Lord Huémac shouted at his guards. "Go and find the man who sells chili peppers and bring him to me!"

The guards rushed out to find the vendor. Even the town crier went to the mountain of Tollán and shouted the message: "Toltecs! Go and look for the Huaxtecan who sells chili peppers! Find him and bring him to our Lord Huémac!"

The entire city of Tollán looked for the chili vendor, but he could not be found. The man had vanished. Most thought he had run away after doing his evil deed, but the following morning he appeared at the same spot where he had been the day before. The guards went rushing to report this to Lord Huémac.

"The chili vendor has appeared!" they cried.

"Bring him at once!" Huémac commanded.

The guards seized the vendor and brought him before Huémac.

"From where do you come?" Huémac asked the man.

"I am a Huaxtecan," the vendor replied. "I sell little chilis."

"You are depraved and wanton," Huémac said. "You come to the marketplace, exposing yourself, frightening our women! Cover yourself. I command you to cover yourself."

"But this is our custom," the Huaxtecan answered. He grinned and Lord Huémac knew he was not dealing with an ordinary man, but with a sorcerer.

"You have bewitched my daughter," Huémac said. "Now you must cure her!" He seized the man and held him tightly. He knew the sorcerer had to be confronted directly and with force, otherwise he would escape and his daughter would remain under his spell.

Then Tezcatlipoca, in the guise of the Huaxtecan, spoke ingratiatingly to Huémac. "My dear Prince," he said. "Why do you assume I can cure your daughter. I am only a chili vendor."

"I will kill you if you don't cure her," Huémac threatened.

"Then if I cure her," the vendor said, "you must promise to give her to me as my wife."

Lord Huémac started back in shock. It would be a disgrace for him to have a Huaxtecan as a son-in-law. All the Toltec nobles would laugh at him. But Huémac thought if his daughter was pregnant and not cured she might give birth to a race of beasts. The vendor was no mere man, he was a sorcerer with destructive powers.

Lord Huémac pondered the situation. He saw how sexual transgressions had brought him to this dilemma. When a man was ruled by the aberrations of sexual desires, he threatened the entire society. Lord Huémac had kept his daughter for himself, and he had been wrong. Now to save her he would have to give her to the sorcerer.

"Very well," Huémac answered. "If you cure her, you may have her as your wife. If you do not, I will have your life."

He turned and ordered his attendants to trim the Huaxtecan's long hair and to bathe him and cover him with sweet oils. When they had bathed and dressed the vendor they brought him before Huémac, and Huémac led him to his daughter's room.

"Look at my daughter," a worried and apprehensive Huémac whispered. "I guarded her, and now she is languishing. Cure her!"

The man gave instructions that he was not to be disturbed. He entered the room and closed the door. Then he lay with Precious Gem in her bed and in a few days she was cured. This is how the sorcerer, Tezcatlipoca, in the guise of a Huaxtecan became the son-in-law of Lord Huémac.

Soon all of Tollán knew the story of how the vendor had come selling chili and stayed to share the bed of Huémac's daughter. The people whispered the story in the marketplace and laughed. Even the nobles laughed and ridiculed Huémac.

"It seems out leader has married his daughter to a common Huaxtecan," the nobles said scornfully.

"Ay, a chili vendor who made her hot," someone would add, and they would all laugh.

Huémac heard the whispers and the scornful laughter, and he cursed and blamed the circumstance on Quetzalcóatl. Huémac was sure that the plot of the chili vendor was the work of the priest. He would not admit that the doings were caused by his own evil sorcerer. He must destroy Quetzalcóatl, but first, he had to get rid of the Huaxtecan.

Huémac took his Captain of War aside and said, "Take the Huaxtecan out on a campaign. Make him a warrior, a Captain, then put him in battle so I can be rid of him."

The Captain went to the Huaxtecan and told him he was now a Captain of the warriors, and he should prepare for the next battle. The sorcerer agreed, but he gathered his own army which consisted of all the deformed dwarfs, cripples and misfits he could find in Tollán. It was a strange band which followed the son-in-law of Huémac out of Tollán. When the Captains of the Jaguar Cult saw his army they laughed and ridiculed him. Who could fight the enemy with such an army. They of course did not know that the man was Tezcatlipoca in disguise.

The armies of the Toltecs marched to Coatepec. There the call to battle was sounded. In the midst of battle, the Toltec Captains withdrew and left the sorcerer and his disreputable army to be taken captive by the enemy.

"Leave the Huaxtecan behind," the War Captain ordered his men. "He will die in battle or be taken captive. We will march directly into Coatepec and be victorious."

The War Captains and their warriors marched to take captives at Coatepec, but the warriors of Coatepec were too strong and they defeated the Toltecs. The Eagle and Jaguar warriors of the Toltecs retreated. To save face, the war captain reported to Lord Huémac that the Huaxtecan and his ludicrous army had been defeated.

Lord Huémac was very angry the battle had been lost, but he rejoiced that he was finally free of the Huaxtecan. Now his precious daughter would be free. But his joy did not last for long. Soon another report came. The runner who came with the message was breathless.

"The Huaxtecan commanded the dwarfs and the cripples," he said. "He fashioned them into an army without fear. They counterattacked the warriors from Coatepec and Zacatepec and destroyed the enemy. The Huaxtecan's army was victorious. Even now they march in victory to Tollán."

Lord Huémac was enraged. The men of Coatepec had beaten his magnificent warriors, and yet the Huaxtecan had defeated the Coatepec warriors with his riffraff army. Any warrior who was victorious in battle had to be welcomed into the city, especially a warrior who defeated the fierce Coatepecans.

Huémac spoke to the nobles. "You shamed the Huaxtecan, and now he is a victorious captain. What do you have to say now?"

"Forgive us, Lord Huémac," the Toltec nobles

said. "Truly now we must receive your son-in-law as a great warrior."

The Toltecs dancing and singing hurried out to greet the victorious army. When they met the Huaxtecan they presented him with a quetzal headdress and a turquoise shield. The shrill flute and the roaring shell trumpet and the barking conch shell announced their entry into Tollán. When they neared the palace they crowned him with plumes and painted his body in yellow and red. They named him a warrior of the Jaguar Cult.

"You have won a great victory for the Toltecs," Lord Huémac said. "I am pleased to call you my son-in-law. Tollán is your home. Come rest your feet at our hearth."

Six

*D*uring the time of Quetzalcóatl's seclusion, the Jaguar Cult gained in power. Huémac and his warriors spread the news that Quetzalcóatl was dead, and they taxed the people heavily, especially the followers of Quetzalcóatl. The precious metals the artisans used in their work were confiscated to pay for the cost of war. Even the bins of corn and other stored foods were taken over by Huémac's warriors. The warriors of the Jaguar Cult held sway over the city of Tollán.

Quetzalcóatl heard reports of the injustices inflicted by the Jaguar Cult. At last he came forth from his seclusion, and went into the streets and talked with the people. The people took courage from his words and began to resist the hated Huémac. The people of Tollán discussed the possibility of peace with their neighbors, and as they gained confidence they talked about an end to Huémac's militaristic rule. The talk enraged Huémac, who swore he would kill Quetzalcóatl, but Quetzalcóatl's followers were so numerous they were able to keep him safe.

"I must destroy Quetzalcóatl," Lord Huémac said, "but his followers protect him too well."

"I have a plan," Tlacahuepan said. "You know that Quetzalcóatl loves his sisters, the stars of the night sky. His sister Quetzalpetlatl is his favorite. Let us pray to Tezcatlipoca that he darken the light of the stars. Thus Quetzalcóatl will suffer greatly and become weak without the love of his sisters."

"Yes," Huémac agreed. "Command the priests of Tezcatlipoca to pray that he darken the night sky." Quetzalcóatl learned of Huémac's evil plan and he hurried to his sister Quetzalpetlatl to warn her of the danger.

"My beloved Quetzalpetlatl," he said to her, "the force of evil on earth reaches across the heavens even to your path to harm you. Come, I will hide you behind Mount Nonohualca; there you will be safe."

"As you wish, my dear brother," Quetzalpetlatl answered. "My only desire is to please you. I will retire there and pray for harmony and peace." So the lustrous and beautiful Quetzalpetlatl was hidden, and Quetzalcóatl retired to his temple to do penance and to fast. He prayed for Ometéotl to restore harmony, and for his own human desire to be subservient to his spirit.

That evening Quetzalcóatl spoke to his brother, a bright star of the western sky. "I need the strength to save Tollán," he said. "The Toltecs are forgetting the teachings of the Ancient Word. I feel their destruction is near if they continue to follow Huémac."

"It is true," his brother replied, "the Toltecs are

turning away from the teachings of Quetzalcóatl. Already many honor our Father Sun by offering him the blood of human sacrifice. One day soon, to ease their guilt, they will call for the sacrifice of a god."

Quetzalcóatl understood what he meant. Yes, the transgressions of the people would continue, the guilt of Tollán would grow. Soon the people would look for a way to assuage their conscience, they would call for the sacrifice of a god. Quetzalcóatl grew sad as he stood in the dusk and contemplated his own death.

In the west the Sun went to bed in the mountains—leaving the Valley of Tula in darkness and reminding the Toltecs that as each day ends so all things end. It was the same night that Huémac met with his Captains of the Jaguar Cult. Dressed in their plumes and paints of war they were a fierce group. Their shields and clubs glistened in the light of the torches. These were the proud warriors of the Toltec Empire, men whose way of life was war. Haughty and disdainful, each man was a tower of strength. The warriors of the Jaguar Cult knew no fear.

"Now is the time to strike fear into our enemies!" Huémac roared and pounded his fist on the table. "Now is the time to bring captives to Tollán, captives we will sacrifice to Huitzilopochtli, our God of War!" The warriors shouted in agreement. Their assent was a shout which came from deep in the chest. Huémac's smile faded as Tlacahuepan whispered in his ear and reminded him that Tollán was not yet ready to support the grand war Huémac had planned. There were many wise men and nobles who followed the teachings of Quetzalcóatl, and they did not see the war as necessary.

"Damn Quetzalcóatl!" Huémac shouted, and his Captains turned to listen. "Is there not a man here who can rid me of that priest?"

The room grew silent. In his rage and hate for Quetzalcóatl, Huémac had thrown down a challenge. Any warrior in the room would face ten enemies to prove his courage, but none could conceive of confronting the priest Quetzalcóatl, much less think of murdering him. The people of Tollán believed Quetzalcóatl was a god, the Plumed Serpent who had brought them corn and wisdom, the Lord of the Dawn who raised the Sun each morning. God or wise man, in their hearts they knew Quetzalcóatl had brought civilization to Tollán. Even the warriors knew this, even they knew that Quetzalcóatl was a power of a higher order of conscience and knowledge. To raise one's club against Quetzalcóatl was like daring to murder the almighty Ometéotl, the Spirit of Duality, the Foundation of the Cosmos.

The warriors shook their heads and turned away. To save their honor they pretended they had not heard the challenge of Huémac. Tlacahuepan quickly stepped forward.

"Perhaps there is a way," Tlacahuepan said. All turned to listen.

"Tell me how to get rid of Quetzalcóatl, and I will make you the chief priest of Tollán," Huémac said.

Tlacahuepan looked at the assembled warriors. "All men, even priests, are vain . . ."

The warriors nodded. They listened.

"It is said even the gods are vain . . ."

Huémac nodded. It was true. Was Tlacahuepan suggesting that even the priest Quetzalcóatl needed assurance and soothing of his vanity, this desire to be more than one's self?

"Go on," Huémac said.

"I have a plan," Tlacahuepan whispered, and drew Huémac aside. "Quetzalcóatl as a man is vain. I will send an artist to make Quetzalcóatl a costume. It will be a magnificent gown, with a headdress of feathers which sweeps to the floor. The beauty of the costume will blind him, he will act like a fool. You will see, his pride and vanity will draw him out."

"Yes," Huémac smiled. "Go on."

"Then we will tell him that as king of the Toltecs he must drink pulque like the Toltecs. It will confuse his senses, he will break his vow as priest. His followers will see he is vain and foolish, and they will no longer follow or protect him."

"Yes!" Huémac nodded. "It is an excellent plan. Make a fool of him and shame him in front of the people, and I will make you chief priest of Tollán!" Huémac raised his bowl of pulque and drank to the completion of the plan. "Now, to our plans for war!" Huémac shouted at his Captains, and they continued their plotting.

In the darkness of the night Tlacahuepan plotted

to bring shame and dishonor to Quetzalcóatl. Tlacahuepan prayed to his gods, Huitzilopochtli, Tezcatlipoca and Toltecatl to help him in his plan. Then he struck a bargain with the artist, Coyotlinahual, who was to go and tempt Quetzalcóatl with a bright and royal costume.

Early the next morning the artist arrived at Quetzalcóatl's temple. This artist who was once a devotee of Quetzalcóatl now sold his talents to the power of darkness to help destroy Quetzalcóatl.

"Lord of the House Made of Dawn," the artist greeted Quetzalcóatl, "I see you have grown weak. Your radiant light is wan. See how your sisters shy away from you, even the beautiful Quetzalpetlatl remains hidden in Mount Nonohualca."

"I have grown old and tired fighting the evil plans of Huémac," Quetzalcóatl answered. "But it is in the nature of all things to grow and wane and then to die. Even my Father the Sun has grown weak and died four times. The Earth and mankind have lived their allotted time, and they too have perished four times. If I am exhausted it is because I struggle daily for the shining light of civilization, I struggle for the grandeur of Tollán."

The artist laughed. "It does not have to be this way," he said.

"No one can break the cycle of ceaseless struggle," Quetzalcóatl said. "Even the gods eventually pass away into oblivion."

"But you yourself taught us that the artist has the

gift of immortality," the artist said proudly. "Man may be born and man may die, but what we shape and fashion will remain for all time."

"That is true," Quetzalcóatl said. He paused for a moment and pondered the words of the artist. Yes, he had taught the artisans and poets that what they shaped and fashioned was the reflection of eternity, as he had taught them that the way to the eternal truth was through song and poetry. Quetzalcóatl yearned for immortality, and his desire to live forever was a grave but human temptation.

"I have seen your light in the morning sky," the artist continued, "and it is weak and dim. But I can make you a costume so bright and radiant that you will glow again with power. Then you will please your followers."

Quetzalcóatl listened, then answered. "It is tempting to think of the power of immortality, the power to work for good. But I must not interfere with the natural cycles of life and death. I cannot change my own destiny."

"It is written in the Ancient Word that both man and god may improve their destiny," the artist said.

"That is true," Quetzalcóatl replied.

"The costume I make for you will be woven of bright quetzal feathers," the artist said. "The headdress will flow across the heavens; it will be woven of the feathers of yellow parrots. Everywhere I will place precious stones, stones so bright and pure they will glisten in the light of the sun. You will be like a new sun rising into the sky, your sisters will be enchanted at the sight of you. You will discover powers you have never known!"

Quetzalcóatl remembered his image in the mirror, he remembered the offer of Huémac and he remembered the beauty of Precious Gem. He remembered that he had not seen his precious sister, Quetzalpetlatl, for a long time. She remained hidden from him. Yes, it was tempting to be as powerful as the sun. It was tempting to think of himself as a glorious, bright god in the heavens of Tollán. Why could he not have new powers to finish his work? Quetzalcóatl anguished over his predicament.

"No, I cannot," he whispered.

In the darkness of his temple, he was tempted. Because he yearned to be as resplendent as the sun in the sky, he was tempted. The cunning artist felt Quetzalcóatl weaken, and he pressed his point.

"Please listen to me, my Lord of the Dawn. There is another reason why you should grow bright with new power. If you had new strength, many new followers would come to you. With your new costume you will light the way for the people of Tollán. They will call you Topiltzin Quetzalcóatl and follow your teachings. For your people you must do this."

"Yes," Quetzalcóatl replied. "For my people I will do this. I must finish my work, I must bring my art and wisdom to them. Go and prepare my costume, artist. Prepare this attire which will make me shine in the House of the Dawn, and which will make me like a Sun in the eyes of my people."

So Quetzalcóatl gave in to the temptations of the false artist, for the love of his people he gave in to the temptation. He had become a man in order to understand human nature, and he had learned how man is ruled by desire. In his heart, Quetzalcóatl harbored the secret desire to have the power of his Father, the Sun.

The artist immediately set to work. With the brightest quetzal feathers he quilted a resplendent gown. The magnificent garment glittered like a serpent's scales in the sun. Then the artist made a mask to cover Quetzalcóatl's face. He made the mask of turquoise. The mouth was made of redshell and the forehead of yellowshell. Serpent fangs were fitted into the mouth to give the mask a fierce aspect, and he added a sweeping beard of cotinga and spoonbill feathers. It was a radiant and glorious costume.

When Quetzalcóatl saw the bright costume flowing in the wind his eyes were bewitched, he was pleased. In years past, when he first came to Tollán, he would not have worn such gaudy attire, but now his desire to be full of new energy had clouded his judgment. His destiny was unraveling as the Lord of Duality had ordained.

"Now Quetzalcóatl is truly the Plumed Serpent of the Dawn," the artist said as he dressed Quetzalcóatl in the seductive garment. Quetzalcóatl looked at himself in the mirror and admired himself.

"How splendid I look," he said. "I am truly renewed. I am the Quetzalcóatl who first came to Tollán. I will show myself to the people."

Quetzalcóatl abandoned his temple and went out into the streets in his new attire. His followers were shocked and dismayed. They had known the Quetzalcóatl who dressed in a plain, cotton gown embroidered with quetzal feathers. Now here was the Lord of the Dawn dressed in a fiery costume which blinded them, and a mask so fierce it frightened the children. The people were apprehensive about the change which had come over Quetzalcóatl, and they withdrew from him.

Now the sorcerers of Tlacahuepan were jubilant that Quetzalcóatl had been tempted from his dark chamber. Now he was vulnerable to the second part of their plan.

Next the sorcerers went to the Place Where Onions Are Washed on Toltec Mountain where they were received by Maxtla, the keeper of the mountain. There they prepared a stew of hot chili, tomatoes, corn, beans and secret herbs which grew on the mountain. They made the stew exceedingly hot, and they planned to feed it to Quetzalcóatl and arouse his carnal desires. They also gathered maguey plants, and in four days they fermented and decanted pulque. They blended wild honey with the pulque so it was sweet to the taste. Then they returned to Tollán and went to Quetzalcóatl's temple, taking with them their stew and pulque.

"We would see your master," the sorcerers said to the attendants, but the attendants were suspicious and would not allow them to enter. Three times the sorcerers pleaded to see Quetzalcóatl.

Then Quetzalcóatl asked, "Where is your home, my grandfathers?"

"We are from Toltec Mountain," the sorcerers replied.

"You may enter," Quetzalcóatl said. "What do you bring?"

"We bring you gifts. A stew for you to eat."

Quetzalcóatl smelled the rich chili stew and it filled him with a great appetite. He felt his nature as a man overcome his nature as a god.

"Why should I eat this hot stew?" he asked.

"It will renew your strength," the sorcerers answered. "You will be pleasing to your sisters."

In this way Quetzalcóatl was tempted again, and he ate the hot stew.

"Now we offer you this pulque," the sorcerers said and offered him the strong wine.

"I must abstain from drink," Quetzalcóatl answered. "Strong drink takes away one's senses. It is fatal."

"This nectar of the gods is sweet," the sorcerers insisted. "It was decanted on Toltec Mountain. It is the drink of the gods. It brings new visions and new powers. You will have new wisdom to share with your followers."

"I will taste it," Quetzalcóatl said.

"Taste it," the sorcerers said.

Quetzalcóatl tasted the sweet pulque, and it was pleasant to his taste. "I will drink one bowlful," he said. He broke his rule of abstinence and drank the libation.

"Quench your thirst," the sorcerers said. "Drink two bowls."

Then, knowing more would make him drunk, they offered him the third bowl, saying: "Drink and make this your libation to your Father, the Sun. Now you are dressed in the dress of a priest of the Sun, you are the Plumed Serpent in your bright plumage. You are strong with chili stew, and you drink the nectar of your Father, the Sun!"

Quetzalcóatl drank the sweet brew and his attendants drank, and they became intoxicated. They went out into the streets singing and dancing.

The people of Tollán were appalled to see Quetzalcóatl and his attendants reveling in the streets, and they felt shame. They turned away and went to hide in their homes. Quetzalcóatl had sinned like a common man, he had broken the rules of the Ancient Word. Now the sins and transgressions of the people of Tollán were on the shoulders of Quetzalcóatl.

When Tlacahuepan reported the event to Huémac, Lord Huémac could not contain his laughter.

"Quetzalcóatl, drunk in the streets!" he shouted. "This brings joy to my heart."

"And the children laughed at him," Tlacahuapan said. "They picked at his feathers as if he were a wet rooster."

Huémac laughed anew, and the warriors of the Jaguar Cult laughed. Quetzalcóatl had been shamed by the sorcerers of their God of War.

"We will celebrate with a feast!" Lord Huémac shrieked. "But first let us do honor to the artist who drew Quetzalcóatl from his hole with that outlandish costume!"

"It is best not to speak of him," Tlacahuepan whispered. "The artist has gone and hanged himself."

"We will celebrate anyway," Huémac said. "Call the musicians and the jugglers and the hunchbacks! Call my Butterfly Woman and her courtesans to come and dance for us! Tell the priests to offer human hearts to Huitzilopochtli. The God of War rules in Tollán!"

The streets of Tollán rang with the merriment of the celebration. In the temples human blood splashed on the once clean altars where before only butterflies and lizards had been offered to the gods. A great throne was built for Lord Huémac, and he sat as ruler of Tollán enjoying the feast. On his right side sat Butterfly Woman, on his left side sat his beautiful daughter. All sang and danced while the terrible odor of human sacrifice filled the streets of Tollán.

Seven

A time of crisis enveloped Tollán. The power of Quetzalcóatl was slipping away, and the people lost faith in him. Huémac continued his wars and the resources he took from the people weakened the social fabric. Vendors and traders from far regions who traveled to Tollán could see the paradox in the society of the Toltecs. There was grandeur and beauty, but at the core there was evil. The temples and the art work of Quetzalcóatl were superb, they had no rival, and yet the armies of Huémac marched daily into the provinces to make war. Quetzalcóatl preached against human sacrifice, but his followers had lost faith. The priests of Huitzilopochtli grew stronger and stronger as they allied themselves with the Jaguar Cult. They offered the hearts of war captives to their gods and to the Sun. The nobles turned away from the teachings of the Ancient Word, forgot the laws and customs of the ancestors, and sought only to gain wealth and take pleasure in women. The poor, left without resources because of the wars, turned to idleness and drink.

Tollán, a great city at its peak of civilization, a society which if it turned toward peace could live in glory, now played conquerer and warmonger and toyed with its own downfall. The traders went away, returning to their lands, and told their stories of the wondrous city of Tollán. They whispered the stories about the priest of Tollán, Quetzalcóatl, he who was the shining star in the House of Dawn, he who had brought the Toltecs civilization. They told of his followers, and how they struggled to keep alive under the harsh rule of Huémac.

The vendors and traders also told about the poverty they saw, and of the nobles who were too busy enjoying their pleasures to help the poor people of the city. It was a strange paradox, the old duality of things, the push and pull which generated energy for all nature. So it was in the society of the Toltecs. The highest aspirations of man, his yearning to learn the truth of the gods through art and poetry vied with the base desires which drew him down into war and sexual pleasures. How would it end? Would harmony come from this push and pull? Or would the great society of the Toltecs fall?

Quetzalcóatl sat in his garden and pondered these same questions. Once he had believed only in the truth of the Ancient Word, and yet he too had fallen, he had taken the drink of the sorcerers, he had fallen as Huémac wished him to fall. What was there in his nature as a man that drew him to desire? And how could he control these desires and show the people the way to truth?

Quetzalcóatl looked at his temple, the highest temple in all of Tollán. He had built the temple so the steps were small and steep, and so each of his attendants who climbed the steps had to meditate on each step. The temple had four chambers, as the universe has four quadrants, and he called the chambers House of Jadestone, House of Gold, House of Redshell, House of Whiteshell. The roof of his house was as the vault of the heavens, a house of turquoise and of quetzal plumes. Daily the Toltecs came to the temple to pray and to listen to the words of Quetzalcóatl. Later, the herald who stood on Crying Out Mountain would call out the words of Quetzalcóatl, and thus the commandments and laws were carried to the outer reaches of the land, even as far as Anáhuac, the place of the eastern waters.

Now as he sat and contemplated, he remembered the arts he had brought to the land of the Toltecs. He had taught the artisans how to cut precious metals, and to the poets and the wise men he had brought art and knowledge. He had even brought new crops to the farmers of the valley: enormous calabash plants, perfectly formed ears of corn, amaranth plants so large they grew as palms, and cotton which grew in many colors. He had also brought scented cacao.

Even the bright birds of many colors had followed Quetzalcóatl into the Valley of Tollán, for the birds were a symbol of the high awareness of spirit he represented. The cotinga, cropendola and the spoonbill were used for their feathers, and their songs filled the city where the poets and wise men gathered to discourse. Even the shops of the artisans were filled with the songs of the birds. The poor people called the birds the songsters of the gods, and Quetzalcóatl was pleased.

But he was not pleased with the nobles who had abandoned the way of the Ancient Word. These people had grown idle as they sought to copy and emulate the social manners of Huémac's palace.

"The nobles grow comfortable and prosperous," Quetzalcóatl said aloud. "They do not see the work which has to be done daily to sustain the spiritual teachings of the Ancient Word. They have left the path of prayer and meditation and penance; now they spend their time in indolence. They have given in to their desires and Huémac fuels those weaknesses to seduce them to his side. The sons and daughters of the noble class have grown fat with abundance. Their sins weigh heavily on the city of Tollán."

Quetzalcóatl heard his own words and despaired. It was true, the rich were leaving the teachings of the ancestors and the wise precepts of the Ancient Word. But hope still lived in the Toltec soul. The young poets and musicians who came to sit with Quetzalcóatl still sang the songs of the ancient teachings. Even now as Quetzalcóatl sat in his garden the young people of the city and from the provinces gathered to sing and to ask questions of their master.

"What do we know of life?" a young man with a flute asked.

"We know we are here but a brief instant," a young woman answered, "then we are gone forever."

"How can we know anything of the eternal truth in our brief life?" the young man asked. All turned to look at their master, Quetzalcóatl.

"Tell us what the ancients taught us of our stay on earth," Quetzalcóatl responded, encouraging the eager young poets who came daily to gain knowledge.

The young man with the flute played a soft melody, the young woman sang.

> "It is not true,
> it is not true
> that we come to this earth to live.
> We come only to sleep,
> only to dream.
>
> Our body is a flower,
> As grass becomes green in the springtime,
> so our hearts will open,
> and give forth buds,
> and then they wither."

Another poet took up the song:

> "Is it true that on earth one lives?
> Not forever on earth,
> only for a little while.
> Though jade it may be, it breaks.
> Though gold it may be, it is crushed.

Though it be quetzal plumes,
it shall not last.
Not forever on earth,
only for a little while."

Then Quetzalcóatl spoke: "For man, life is a
shadow, a dream. He yearns for the truth in his soul,
and he is on earth but for a brief time. The ancients
recorded four ages of time on earth, and each age
was destroyed. There is no truth in an earth which
ends, in gods which die, there can only be an answer
in Ometéotl, the Foundation of the Cosmos. Only in
Ometéotl is there an answer. But man is blinded by
life, he cannot see the eternal truth resting at the
navel of the world, he cannot see the foundation
which sustains the universe. He cannot see, but he
expresses his yearnings for the truth in poetry. These
songs and flowers are a way to the truth."

The young poets nodded. They knew that no one
could know the real truth on earth, and they knew
that good men and women yearned for the eternal
truth. Their ancestors had known parts of the great,
eternal truth, and they had recorded their thoughts
in the teachings of the Ancient Word. They knew
that parts of the truth could be found through the
language of poetry and song. This language of metaphor, this language of flowers and song was the language used to express truth. And so the poet sang:

"Eagerly does my heart yearn for flowers.
I suffer with songs, yet I create them on earth.

I crave flowers that will not perish in my hands!
Where might I find lovely flowers, lovely songs?
Such as I seek, spring does not produce on earth."

Quetzalcóatl also sang:

"My poets, my priests, I ask you.
From whence come the flowers that enrapture man?
The songs that intoxicate, the lovely songs?"

Another poet took up the song and answered:

"Only from His home do they come, from the
        innermost part of the heaven
              only from there come
        the myriad of flowers.
Where the nectar of the flower is found
        the fragrant beauty of
              the flower is refined . . .
They interlace, they interweave,
        among them sings,
              among them warbles the quetzal bird."

Quetzalcóatl completed the song:

"The flowers sprout, they are fresh, they grow.
They open their blossoms,
And from within emerge the flowers of song.
Among men Ometéotl scatters them,
He sends them.
He is the singer!"

All nodded and bowed at the end of the song, all were happy. That was the way of the Toltecs, to arrive at truth through song and poetry. Now the discourse was ended, the young poets moved on, waving goodbye to the priest Quetzalcóatl. Quetzalcóatl was pleased. Divine inspiration was the way to eternal truth. Ometéotl was the singer, he was the foundation of the universe, his voice was the wind which reverberated in the songs of man. This is what he had taught the Toltecs. Then Quetzalcóatl frowned because he knew many still left the true way and followed the example of Huémac.

Quetzalcóatl rose quickly and went to his bath. There he prayed for the Toltecs and for all of mankind, then he bled the flesh of his shinbone in penance. He walked alone in the dark of night and bathed himself at the Place Where Turquoises Are Washed. It was now dark and Tollán slept, but Quetzalcóatl did not sleep; he was a vigilant star which circled the earth while man slept. He meditated and did penance and waited to light the morning sky for his Father the Sun.

But Huémac did not meditate, nor did he do penance. Huémac did not sleep. He spent his time carousing in the chambers of Butterfly Woman, drinking pulque and feasting. As was usual, when he drank he ranted and raved against Quetzalcóatl. Once he had blamed Quetzalcóatl because he had refused the offer of his daughter; now he blamed him because he thought Quetzalcóatl had caused the loss of his daughter to the Huaxtecan. But in his heart

Huémac hated Quetzalcóatl because they were opposites, and that which was ignorant and savage in Huémac's nature drove him to destroy that which was wise and noble in Quetzalcóatl.

"Our wars would bring us tribute and many captives if only Quetzalcóatl would not interfere!" Huémac roared in his drunkenness. "He aids the enemy and he hampers our effort!"

The warriors also cursed Quetzalcóatl. They too hated the priest of peace. Butterfly Woman whispered in Huémac's ear: "You must get Quetzalcóatl with a woman, then he will fall and the people of Tollán will drive him from the land."

"Yes," Huémac said. "But the priest has no time for women; he spends his time teaching the Ancient Word and exhorting the people to peace with their neighbors. Let us frighten the people first, and save your suggestion for later," Huémac said. He called his sorcerer Tlacahuepan.

"My Lord," Tlacahuepan answered the call, instantly at Huémac's side.

"You promised us you would destroy Quetzalcóatl, and the priest still walks the streets of Tollán. The people have forgotten he was vain and intoxicated as one of them. What can you do?"

Tlacahuepan said, "I can cause, with the help of the God of War and Tezcatlipoca, many evil things to come to the Toltecs. Then they will blame Quetzalcóatl for their ill luck. But you have to will it, my Lord, you have to pray to Tezcatlipoca for the downfall of Quetzalcóatl."

"I will do it gladly," Huémac answered. "In the past you have shown us the power of your sorcery. Now go to the marketplace, and instigate unrest among the people. Put fear in their hearts."

In the morning, Tlacahuepan, whose heart was dark and rotten with the most abominable sins, went and sat in the center of the market square. He took with him a small manikin which he caused to dance on his hand. This manikin was none other than Huitzilopochtli, the War God. The Toltecs were amazed to see this feat of magic. They came running to see the show of the dancing manikin, but even as they pressed forward many were trampled and crushed.

Tlacahuepan laughed when he saw the panic he had created. He taunted the Toltecs and shouted: "Look at the magic I create! I am so powerful you cannot kill me! I dare you to kill me!"

The frightened Toltecs stoned Tlacahuepan, and he was crushed by the stoning. The Toltecs thought they had rid the city of the sorcerer, but in a short time the corpse began to give off an awful stench. The wind carried the stench of death and the people who breathed it died. The city was gripped with fear. In their once glorious marketplace, the center of commerce for their empire, the rotting corpse lay, giving off the deadly stench. The people prayed and cried for help. They prayed to the god Tezcatlipoca for help, not realizing that it was Tezcatlipoca who gave Tlacahuepan the power to do his evil.

"Get rid of the corpse," Tezcatlipoca told the Toltecs. "Go and tie it with ropes and pull it away."

The Toltecs went with ropes and trussed the stinking corpse and tried to pull it away, but they could not move it.

The Toltecs cried. "How is it that many men cannot move one corpse. Are our sins this heavy?"

It was true, the transgressions of the Toltecs were embodied in the rotting corpse. Many were the transgressions of Tollán. The city fell to crying and grieving over its sins. Again they tried to remove the corpse of Tlacahuepan. All the men went with ropes, and they sang to gather strength.

"Work together, Toltecs! Together to rid the evil of our city!"

They pulled with all their strength, but the ropes broke and those who held the ropes fell and some were killed. Many brave men of Tollán were killed, and the women grieved.

"We cannot move the corpse," they cried to the dark god Tezcatlipoca, and he gave them a new song to sing.

"Sing this song," he told them. "We pull this human log, Tlacahuepan, the human owl!"

The people were full of fear when they heard these words. The human log was the sorcerer Tlacahuepan, and his sin was the sin of incest. Tlacahuepan was rotten throughout.

The people cried, but they took courage. Singing the new song they pulled at the corpse again, and this time the corpse began to stir. But again the ropes broke and the human log rolled over the people and crushed many to death.

Finally Tezcatlipoca told the people he would give them the strength to remove the corpse, but only if they admitted the evil had come to the Toltecs because of Quetzalcóatl's transgression. The people recognized the sorcery, but still many agreed and blamed Quetzalcóatl for the rotting corpse and the deaths it caused.

"Quetzalcóatl is to blame for this," some cried as they removed the corpse and threw it away. Others drank to forget the evil and pretended they had not seen the evil of the sorcerer.

The followers of Quetzalcóatl resisted the accusations. "It is not our Topiltzin Quetzalcóatl who does us evil. All of you can clearly see that this deed was the work of the sorcerer, Tlacahuepan. He is a magician, even when it appears we have killed him he does not die."

And so the people were divided, and because they needed someone to blame, some continued to speak out against Quetzalcóatl. They accused him of not coming to their assistance, when in truth no one had prayed to the god of light, Quetzalcóatl.

When the day's events were reported to Huémac he laughed with satisfaction. Finally the power of Quetzalcóatl was being broken; the people were being divided. When Quetzalcóatl's followers became weak and divided and could no longer protect their priest, then Huémac would use Butterfly

Woman's advice. Until then, he would continue sending Tlacahuepan out to do his evil deeds, to spread panic and fear among the people. Once the people were stirred up and full of fear, they would lose their common sense. They would blame Quetzalcóatl for the evil in the city of Tollán. They would turn to Huémac, and they would give him supreme power.

"Go once again," Huémac said to Tlacahuepan, "and do this. . . . "

Eight

lacahuepan, dressed as a valiant warrior in yellow parrot feathers, went to the marketplace. Carrying a big drum, prancing and dancing like a trickster he entered. The people heard his drum beat and they flocked to him like ants to honey.

"Why are you sad, people of Tollán," he sang. "Be happy! You were victorious over your enemies of Coatepec and Zacatepec. Now you should sing and dance to celebrate your victory."

The Toltecs rushed to Yellow Feather Man. His music drew them like the magic drum of a shaman draws the souls of men. Soon there was a large crowd gathered. Even Huémac appeared, with his sad daughter at his side.

"Yellow Feather Man tells the truth," Huémac said. "It is a time to celebrate. Let the crier call out from Crying Out Mountain, and let all our young people celebrate the fiesta and follow the musician."

The crier went to the top of the mountain and called the people to the celebration. From everywhere the Toltecs came. The sorcerer sang and beat his drum, and the people swayed to the beat. They were entranced by the music of the sorcerer. Great throngs of young men and women followed the sorcerer out of the city to the Place of Rock Cliffs.

"Follow our champion with the drum, follow the song of his drum," the people cried.

Leaping and turning they followed him. Dancing back to back and belly to belly they went. They were entranced by the song and drunk on the pulque of the fiesta. They lost their minds to the rapture of the song and to the desire in their bodies, and there at that wild gathering the young men and women committed many sins.

The sorcerer invented the song as he beat his drum, and the young men and women took it from his lips and it became their song. Full of the fever in their bodies they danced at the Place of Rock Cliffs, the Place of Crags. In their ecstasy many people fell into the deep ravine and died. All who fell onto the crags were turned to stone.

The sorcerer led the celebrants over a bridge of stone, then he caused the bridge to break and many fell into the water and also were turned into stones. The beat of the drum and the songs of the sorcerer rose to a feverish pitch, and as the singing continued, the deaths continued. Only one, an old man who had not sung the song of Yellow Feather Man, escaped. He saw the awful dance and the people turned to stones and he ran to tell Quetzalcóatl what was happening.

Quetzalcóatl went with the old man to the Place of the Cliffs. The place was deserted and still. Yellow Feather Man was gone, his fitful song and dance were done. Only piles of stones and boulders filled the deserted place.

"There," the old man pointed. "See the rocks. Look at the shapes of the rocks," he said and wept, for he recognized many of the townspeople frozen in death.

Quetzalcóatl also wept. He had come too late to help his people. He knew that Huémac was planning many evil deeds to turn the people against him, and because he could not be everywhere the sorcerers continued their work. If only the people could see that it was Huémac and his hate and anger which lay behind the sorcery, they themselves could stop Huémac. But the people were superstitious and easily tricked. They believed in the power of Huémac's false sorcerers, they had lost faith in the teachings of the Ancient Word.

"They followed Yellow Feather Man," the old man said. "They did not see that it was Huémac and his sorcerer who entangled their thoughts."

"Yes," Quetzalcóatl said sadly. "Those who now follow the way of war and evil pleasures have their hearts turned to stone. They have lost the goodness in their hearts."

So Quetzalcóatl went out among the people and told them they themselves could resist the evil which came to Tollán. "Believe in your strength as good persons, believe in the good rules of the Ancient

Word. Do not allow evil thoughts to take your hearts, do not follow the path of war."

Many heard him, and they were made strong by the teachings of the Ancient Word. Others chose not to listen, and they were obedient to Huémac, their earthly ruler. They would not admit that Huémac sacrificed some of them to turn the rest against Quetzalcóatl.

The sorcerer Tlacahuepan laughed at the ruin he had caused. "I will bring the Toltecs to their knees, I will deliver them to the God of War!" he boasted.

Again he dressed as a warrior, and he told the crier to summon the common people and the farmers.

"Tell the people to come to Xochitlan to work the chinampa," he said. "Tell them they shall reap much food."

Famine and the wars had depleted the food of the Toltecs, so the people went running to Xochitlan. But when the people were gathered at Xochitlan, the sorcerer turned and slew them with his club. He had promised food, he delivered death. Xochitlan, the Place of Flowers, became the place of death. Right and left the sorcerer grabbed the people and crushed their heads.

Some ran to escape the wrath of the sorcerer, but even as they ran they trampled each other and were crushed to death. The Place of Flowers ran red with their blood.

Many other signs and omens appeared in Tollán, and the people went to Quetzalcóatl so he might interpret the signs. They prayed the curses of the sorcerers be lifted, but it was too late. The sins of Tollán were too great. Already omens predicted the fall of Tollán. Still the people gathered in small numbers at the temple of Quetzalcóatl.

"Forgive us," the people cried. "We are afraid. We have left the way of wisdom and the teachings of the Ancient Word. Now evil signs predict our doom."

"Tell me what you have seen," Quetzalcóatl said.

A spokesman for the group stepped forward and spoke.

"We have seen a white hawk, its head pierced by an arrow. The white hawk came flying and swooping low over the land of the Toltecs. It flew as if it were dying."

Quetzalcóatl was grieved and he answered: "The death of the sun is coming. The sun will no longer shine over Tollán."

Then the people wept and pulled their hair in anguish. What they feared most, the death of the sun was coming. When the sun died, the end of the Fifth Age of Mankind would die, everyone would die in a terrible cataclysm.

"There is another sign," the spokesman said. "Last night we saw the mountain on fire. The mountain we call Grass Mountain was burning. The flames rose into the dark sky."

Quetzalcóatl wept, then he spoke: "The death of the earth is coming. No longer will the earth give sustenance to the people of Tollán. We have poisoned the earth with our wrongdoings. Our food will be bitter as the earth dies."

Then in great sadness Quetzalcóatl retired to his temple to pray and fast. He had explained the signs, and now he retired to meditate on their destiny. The people remained weeping and waiting for Quetzalcóatl to return.

"Now we know the end is coming," the spokesman said. "It is written that all things must pass, and we are on this earth only to dream. We forgot the good teachings of his widsom, and now the Toltec way is passing. Who will remember us when we are gone? Who will say we lived in peace with the earth and our neighbors? Who will remember the people of Tollán?"

Few would remember the good people of Tollán, but many would know of the terrible things which happened in the land of the Toltecs. A dry spell came and there was no rain for the crops. Tláloc, the God of Rain, would not grant the prayers of the Toltecs. He would not send rain to bless the fields. The food of the Toltecs turned bitter and rotten. Sweltering heat and great clouds of dust came, blotting out the light of the sun. The wind burned everything. Then stones began to rain from the sky, which destroyed crops and injured people. The land of the Toltecs was devastated by the rain of stones, the people rushed wildly into the streets, lamenting their suffering.

And still the evil signs did not abate. In the middle of the city a huge, sacrificial altar descended from the sky. Many went to the altar to pray, but they lost their lives. The altar was the work of dark cosmic

forces, the forces which conspired to dominate Quetzalcóatl.

Now the God of Fear swept through the land. The
Toltecs lost their courage and hope. Their children
suffered from hunger, the old and the infirm died.
Everywhere there was hunger, everywhere there was
death. No one could eat the food of the poisoned
earth.

"Deliver us from our misery!" the people prayed,
but there was no help for those who had turned
away from the path of harmony, peace and wisdom.

The shrill cry of despair filled Tollán. Funeral pyres
were lit and burned day and night. The city became a
city of ghosts. The guant figures of the starving
Toltecs roamed the streets, gray smoke rose into the
night sky. For the Toltecs, the end of the dream of
Tollán was near.

In the night the sad, piercing cry of flutes filled the
city. The people chanted the songs of death. The
Lord and lady of Mictlan walked in the streets, death
was everywhere. In desperation the people gathered
around the palace of Lord Huémac and cried for
help.

"Help us, Lord Huémac," they cried as they held
their dead children in their arms.

Lord Huémac appeared. His face was swollen and
his eyes were dark from pulque. The people saw him
and were frightened. Huémac was the image of death
itself. But the people needed help, and so the spokesman for the multitude spoke.

"We seek your help, Lord Huémac. We ask your

help. The sorcerers deceive and trick the people of Tollán, they kill and murder our old and our young. The stench of death fills Tollán, and we have nothing to eat. Neighbor turns against neighbor for a scrap of food. The food goes to feed the soldiers, and the wars continue, but here at home we are starving, here at home everything is rotten. We beg for your help. We ask your help."

"What would you have me do?" Huémac asked angrily.

"You are our leader," the spokesman answered. "You must cleanse the city of this evil. You must make peace with our neighbors to the south, not war. If you do not root out the evil which plagues our land, then Tollán will die, the Toltecs will die."

"Don't blame me for your misery!" Huémac shouted. "I have made proper sacrifices to the Sun and to the God of War. Human blood marks my temple. If someone is to blame for the misery and weakness of Tollán, it is Quetzalcóatl! Yes, those who have followed him have brought this misery to Tollán."

Huémac paused; the people were listening. Finally the people of Tollán were listening. His plan had worked. He had induced fear and strife into the society, and now they had turned to him for help. Now he could demand the banishment of Quetzalcóatl. No, he would ask for more, he would demand the sacrifice of Quetzalcóatl. Yes, the masses always looked for a scapegoat, they always needed someone to blame. Let it be Quetzalcóatl!

Huémac proceeded cautiously. "Don't you see, my
fellow Toltecs. The sin and guilt you speak of is not
yours, it belongs to Quetzalcóatl. He is a false priest,
he says we need no human sacrifice to give the sun
its energy, he preaches we should take no captives for
the sacrifices. That is why we have grown weak. He
has caused our weakness, and as he is the cause of all
our misery, he must be sacrificed to cleanse the city
and please the gods!"

Huémac shouted his last words and they went to
the heart of the people like a burning spear. The people trembled. What would it mean to sacrifice Quetzalcóatl? He was Lord of the Dawn, Messenger of
the Father Sun. If he were sacrificed, would he hide
his face in the western mountains and rise no more
into his House of Dawn? And if he were not there,
would the sun rise?

Huémac allowed a moment of thought, then he
pressed his demand. "We must make a sacrifice to
appease the gods. Quetzalcóatl has angered the gods
by not giving them the energy of life, the blood they
demand. The gods will return the strength and
power to Tollán only if Quetzalcóatl is sacrificed!"

The people of Tollán grew still, frozen by the fear
they felt in their hearts. The Toltecs bowed their
heads in shame. It was true, a sacrifice was needed,
the angry gods needed to be appeased. But Quetzalcóatl had done no wrong. He had brought art and
civilization to the Toltecs, and he had brought them
corn and other foods. He had made Tollán great, he
had made it the center of all Mexico. Now Lord

Huémac blamed him for the evil in Tollán, and asked for his sacrifice. How could this be? The people turned to their spokesman.

The spokesman bowed and stepped forward. "We cannot sacrifice our Dear Prince Quetzalcóatl. He has brought us our civilization, he has raised us from living like animals to living like men. He has brought us the wisdom of our ancestors, the teachings of the Ancient Word."

Huémac sputtered with anger as he lost control of the crowd. They still respected Quetzalcóatl. "Imbeciles! Idiots!" he shouted. "Don't you understand that without this sacrifice there is no hope!"

At that moment Huémac felt a hand on his arm. He turned to see Tlacahuepan.

"Calm yourself, my Lord," Tlacahuepan said. "Do not drive the people away. They are very near to accepting this sacrifice, but they need to see Quetzalcóatl sin before they will sacrifice him. There is one way, use the advice given to you by Butterfly Woman."

Tlacahuepan smiled, and turned toward Butterfly Woman. She returned the smile of the sorcerer, she who had sold herself into his service. Now she ruled in the house of Huémac, and Lady Huémac was the abandoned wife.

They were right, Huémac nodded. He composed himself and turned to face the crowd. "Very well," he said. "You say Quetzalcóatl has not sinned. But what if I tell you he has committed the most terrible sin against the teachings of the Ancient Word? Would you then sacrifice him?"

The crowd grew silent. Not a breath stirred as they thought about the portent in Huémac's words. Yes, there could be no doubt that if Quetzalcóatl sinned against the Ancient Word then he was a false priest, a false god. He would have to be sacrificed. Even the spokesman said this as he spoke.

"Yes, Lord Huémac. If our Dear Prince Quetzalcóatl sinned against the Ancient Word, then he should be banished from the land of the Toltecs, nay, he should be sacrificed so that the gods will smile on us once again."

"The people of Tollán have spoken," Huémac shouted. "The fate of Quetzalcóatl rests with the Toltecs. I will prove to you that he has sinned."

Then Huémac turned and conferred with Butterfly Woman and with Tlacahuepan. Butterfly Woman was to take a love potion to Quetzalcóatl's sister, which would fill her mind and heart with carnal desire. Tlacahuepan would go the temple of Quetzalcóatl and induce him to drink pulque, saying it would give him the power to save the crumbling Toltec Empire. With this plan, they would bring the downfall of Quetzalcóatl.

"Look into the morning sky," were the last words Huémac said to the people. "There you shall see the sin of Quetzalcóatl."

Nine

Now Tlacahuepan summoned the gods Tezcatlipoca and Totecatl, and together they went dressed as priests to the temple of Quetzalcóatl. In the gloom of the night they went to plot his downfall. What they did not know was that Quetzalcóatl knew they were coming and awaited their arrival. The destiny of Quetzalcóatl had been foretold, and so the god knew how his days in Tollán would end. He knew that in the year One Reed he would return to the eastern waters from whence he came, and the year One Reed had now returned. His work among the Toltecs was done. He had brought them a shining civilization, it was now up to them to revive and nurture it. Only thus could they harvest the fruits of wisdom.

At the door of the temple the sorcerers called out. "We bring a sacrament to the Lord Quetzalcóatl," they said. The sacrament they spoke of was a magical drink so intoxicating that those who partook lost their senses. With this drink the sorcerers planned to enflame the carnal desires of Quetzalcóatl.

Two times they asked permission to enter, and two times the cautious attendants, the dwarfs of Quetzalcóatl, refused them. The third time Quetzalcóatl told his attendants to allow the sorcerers entry.

"Lord Quetzalcóatl," Tlacahuepan said. "As you know, Tollán will fall from greatness the moment you leave us. Now we need your strength and guidance. We have prepared this libation to fill you with new strength. Partake and you will grow strong, you will receive new visions, you will be pleasing to your sister who now hides from you. This sweet pulque is the sacrament of the gods. If you leave the Toltecs will fall into misery, they will not remember the wise teachings of Quetzalcóatl."

All this the sorcerers said in a very flattering language. They offered him the sweet wine, three times they offered it.

Quetzalcóatl grieved for their sins and treachery. He was not fooled by the sorcerers, he recognized his old enemies: Tezcatlipoca, Huitzilopochtli, Toltecatl and Tlacahuepan. These gods of darkness, war, wine and the sorcerer Tlacahuepan had brought much suffering to his people. Huémac had used them to weaken the Toltecs. Quetzalcóatl knew that when he left, the society, the arts and the knowledge of the Toltecs, would be destroyed. In a short time everything would be lost. And why? The people had listened to Huémac and his false gods, and they had forgotten the true teachings of the Ancient Word.

Now Quetzalcóatl understood why in the legends he had been called the Lord Redeemer—it was part of his destiny to take the transgressions of the Toltecs into his heart. He had become a man to understand the heart of the Toltec people. Quetzalcóatl did not fear his enemies, he understood their role in the continuous tension between good and evil, and the duality of light and darkness.

Knowing this, Quetzalcóatl took the bowl of nectar the sorcerers offered. They nodded in approval.

"Drink," they entreated him.

"I take the libation," Quetzalcóatl answered. "But I do not drink because you offer it. I drink to lose my senses as the Lord of the Dawn, I drink so I can fall to the ground like a man. As I fall, I renew myself, as I am reborn so are my people. My destiny has come full cycle. I am ready to accept it."

The sorcerers did not understand his words, but they were pleased to see him partake of the pulque which would confuse his senses. On Mount Nonohualca, they knew, Butterfly Woman was at this moment preparing Quetzalcóatl's sister so that she might be ready for her brother.

Quetzalcóatl raised the bowl and drank. As he tasted the sweetened drink he thought of the red and gold sun which set in the west. The sun was dying, the earth was dying, the Toltec civilization was dying, and even the Plumed Serpent was preparing to die. Who would greet the Father Sun in the morning? Who would be there to light the way for the Sun to warm the earth?

He thought of the arts and wisdom he had brought his beloved people. Time would move in its predestined cycle, and everything would disappear in its flux. Only the words would remain, the songs and poetry. And who in the future could translate the songs to arrive at the ancient knowledge?

As he drank he was filled with great sadness. History would record his fall, history would proclaim how the Lord of the Dawn fell to earth to infuse his consciousness in mankind. But would the future remember his days as a teacher of art and knowledge? Would people remember that his meditations reached the highest sphere of vision in his search for the eternal truth?

"Drink and be joyous!" the sorcerers sang. They anticipated his fall and knew he would soon depart Tollán. Huitzilopochtli was bold enough to begin the song of departure.

> "House of quetzal,
> House of quetzal,
> Of zacuan, of redshell,
> I leave thee now."

Quetzalcóatl drank and became confused. He asked his priests and attendants to partake of the strong drink, and soon the temple was filled with despair. Huémac came to the temple, and sought out Quetzalcóatl. They looked at each other.

"My old enemy," Quetzalcóatl said. "You have come to see my downfall."

"Yes," Huémac boasted. "For many years I have planned your destruction. Finally with you gone, I will be in command! But sing and be joyous, enjoy your last days on earth. Doesn't the Ancient Word tell us we are here but for a moment, we are here only to dream. So let our dreams be sweet!" He laughed sarcastically. Even at this moment he was cruel to the god Quetzalcóatl.

"Come with me," Huémac said, and stumbling in the dark he led Quetzalcóatl through the dark passageway to the top of the temple. The sun had set, the stars glittered in the sky.

"See there," Huémac pointed. "The morning star has now become the evening star. It is to the west, ready to bed for the night, ready to disappear into the western mountains. And, see the beautiful sisters of Quetzalcóatl, shining in all their glory. Such beauty must be tasted to be appreciated. Tonight is a night when the heavens will be askew, the stars will be in strange conjunctions. Call the beautiful Quetzalpetlatl, your favorite sister who hides behind Mount Nonohualca. She yearns to see her brother, she yearns to wish him goodbye as he begins his journey. Call her! Call her down to the evening star!"

This was Huémac's challenge, this was his plan to bring Quetzalcóatl to his ultimate transgression. Again, Quetzalcóatl understood that Huémac meant him only evil. It was not that Huémac had won the struggle of many years, it was that the time had come for Quetzalcóatl's destiny and life to enter a new stage. It was time for Quetzalcóatl to return to the House Made of Dawn, the realm of the gods. But before he left, he had to take the sins of mankind into his soul. That is why he would call his sister to his temple which was now defiled. He was destined to sin as a man might sin before he returned to his house in the heavens.

He looked into the heavens where the stars glittered in all their beauty. His sisters, his lovely sisters. All called to him, all looked at the evening star who readied for bed on the western horizon. Only his favorite sister he did not see, only Quetzalpetlatl was hidden behind Mount Nonohualca where he had sent her.

Quetzalcóatl turned to his attendants and said, "Go and bring my sister, Quetzalpetlatl, so she may join me on this my day of departure, so she may say goodbye to her brother."

The attendants did his bidding, and hurried to Mount Nonohualca and spoke to Quetzalpetlatl.

"Beloved sister of Quetzalcóatl," they said, "our dear and penitent lady. The Lord of the Dawn calls for you to be with him tonight."

"I will go to him," the beautiful Quetzalpetlatl answered.

And so, in the night sky over Tollán, the stars moved into new positions, new conjunctions with the evening star, he who was also the morning star. The priests who watched the skies nightly saw this, and they were filled with fear. The bright star Quetzalpetlatl moved to the western horizon to be with her brother, Quetzalcóatl. Never before in the memory of the priests who watched the stars had Quetzalcóatl and his sister bedded together. This was a sign of the god, an age had come to an end. In the temple the sorcerers laughed and sang the song of the drunkard to Quetzalcóatl and his sister.

> "Where now is your home
> Dear sister Quetzalpetlatl?
> The night sky is dark,
> You and your brother are hidden.
> Your home is now here,
> In the bowl of pulque!"

Then the sorcerers left, leaving Quetzalcóatl and his sister alone. Night fell and in the sky the sister stars shivered with fear as the two bright stars on the western horizon disappeared into the western mountains.

When Quetzalcóatl awoke he was filled with remorse. His sister awakened with him, and she too was full of shame.

"Oh, unfortunate me," Quetzalcóatl cried. "Now I know the heart of man, now I have fallen in sin. I must leave Tollán." He was no longer the unblemished morning star; he had succumbed to the temptations of desire so that he could know the heart of mankind. His destiny was being completed in its appropriate time. He raised his voice and sang his song of departure.

> "No more will the days
> Be counted in my home.

For it shall be empty.
Only beyond will I awaken.
From this earth, from this flesh,
I depart.
From desire and pain
I depart.
Never more will I thrive,
My mother will know me no more.
My mother, Coatlicue,
She of the Serpent Skirt,
Oh Holy One,
My Earth Mother,
I, your child, am weeping."

His attendants heard his song of departure, and
they grieved. Their Dear Lord was going away, he
was leaving forever. The attendants wept and sang.

"No more will we delight in him,
Our noble, Quetzalcóatl.
No more thy precious crown!
The bleeding thorns will be broken!
We will mourn him,
We weep for him, our Dear Prince."

When their lament was done, Quetzalcóatl spoke
to them, saying: "Desire caused my death, as it is the
death of man. I now know how man is led to sin,
and so when I return I will know how to redeem his
virtue. But now I must depart. First, I must lie in
darkness for four days, I must visit the Lord and

Lady of Mictlan for four days. Go and prepare a funeral urn, and lay my body in it."

A funeral urn was brought, made of gold and precious stones. The attendants and priests placed Quetzalcóatl in the dark urn; then all of his followers went into mourning. The people knew that after his death Quetzalcóatl would disappear from the sky for four days and nights. They knew that now Quetzalcóatl would descend into Mictlan, the Land of the Dead. He would dwell in the Land of the Dead four days and four nights, and when he returned he would begin his journey to the eastern waters.

The next morning all of Tollán knew of the fall of Quetzalcóatl. No business was transacted in the marketplace, the vendors gathered only to listen to the reports of the priests who had watched the night sky. From the temple came the sounds of wailing as the priests of Quetzalcóatl mourned their master and prayed for him as he journeyed to the Land of the Fleshless Ones. It was true, the Dear Prince Quetzalcóatl was dead.

A great cry of mourning filled the city of Tollán. Shrieks of grief filled the air, the men broke their war clubs and covered themselves with ashes, the women tore their hair and went crying into the streets. The Toltecs knew that Quetzalcóatl had died for their sins, he had loved his people so dearly he had given up his own life for them. ❧

"Our beloved Prince is dead!" the people cried in the streets. Covered with ashes and singing the songs of mourning, the long lines of mourners gathered around the Temple of Quetzalcóatl to view the great urn which held the earthly body of their Dear Prince. Even from the provinces the people came, from the farms in the valley the people came to pay homage to their dead prince. From all the tribes of Mexico the rulers and nobles sent emissaries to Tollán. Even neighbors upon whom Huémac had made war came to pay their final respects to the great teacher of wisdom. It seemed all of the world knew that Quetzalcóatl had died, and Tollán was filled with mourners.

Then the grief of the Toltecs turned to anger. The people finally realized that it was Huémac who had driven Quetzalcóatl to death. It was Huémac and his evil which had caused the fall of the Lord of Dawn. The angry crowd grew and swelled as it moved towards Huémac's palace, where at that very moment Huémac toasted the death of Quetzalcóatl.

"The people are coming here," his servants reported.

Huémac smiled. Yes, he thought, the people of Tollán were finally coming to him, to honor him and give him their allegiance.

When Huémac saw the multitude moving toward his palace, he went out to greet the people. He believed they came to make him king. He did not realize they came with anger in their hearts.

"My dear Toltecs," Huémac shouted. "You know that Quetzalcóatl has died because of his sins. Now the days of grandeur will return to Tollán! I am your

Prince, I will be your victorious captain in the battles with our enemies!"

"You are to blame for the death of Quetzalcóatl!" the people cried in anger.

Huémac did not understand. He thought they came to make him their king. Now he looked at their angry faces, and he saw that they blamed him. They turned against him and with anger in their faces and stones in their hands the multitude surrounded Huémac and his attendants.

"It is you who have brought us to ruin!" the spokesman of the people cried. "Your wars have bled us dry, your madness has turned neighbor against neighbor, and now you have plotted with your evil sorcerers the death of our Lord of the Dawn! You have caused the death of him who brought us art and wisdom!"

"I am innocent!" Huémac shouted. He turned and called for his guards, but his warriors did not respond; to save themselves they had deserted him.

"I am innocent!" Huémac cried, and he turned to Tlacahuepan for help. "Explain to them that I had nothing to do with the death of Quatzalcóatl!"

Tlacahuepan bowed and stepped forward to face the huge crowd. Tlacahuepan shouted. "Who is responsible for the death of Quetzalcóatl?"

"Huémac!" the people shouted in one cry.

"Then to atone for his death you need a sacrifice!" Tlacahuepan answered.

Huémac could not believe what he heard. Even as

the great shout "Sacrifice Huémac" filled the air, he knew he had been betrayed by the treacherous Tlacahuepan.

He turned and grabbed at Tlacahuepan, "No," he said. "You have misled the people! Explain to them—" He said no more. Tlacahuepan only smiled. In his eyes Huémac saw the treachery. Now he knew it had been planned all along; he, Huémac, had been used by the destructive forces of human nature. He had been deceived, as he had deceived Quetzalcóatl.

"I can explain!" Huémac shouted to the people. And again the cry rose, "Sacrifice Huémac!"

Huémac turned to run as the first stones fell. There was nowhere to go. He called for his guards, but there was no response, there would be no help. A stone hit his head and drew blood. Huémac fell to the ground; the shower of stones pelted his body as the angry crowd surrounded him. Even Tlacahuepan lifted a stone to throw at his master. The once mighty Huémac, leader of the Jaguar Cult, now lay like a commoner, dying in the dust of the street.

"I was wrong, I was wrong," Huémac cried as he lay dying. "I took my strength from the gods of destruction and they deceived me. I sold my soul to darkness to destroy the wisdom of Quetzalcóatl, and this is my reward. I gave myself to the evil pleasures and desires of the body, and those moments are of no comfort at my death. I drank to feel like a warrior god, and the pulque only confused my thoughts and led me down a senseless path. I wanted to be King of the Toltecs, Emperor of all the lands of Mexico, wealthy, powerful, and for that I plotted against Quetzalcóatl. I drove him to his death. It is ended. The dream is ended. . . . "

When Huémac was dead the angry multitude drew around his body. They had found some measure of atonement for the grief and frustration they felt, but they realized that killing Huémac was not the answer.

"The gods forgive us," the spokesman said, "now there is fresh blood on our hands. Truly we have broken the teachings of the Ancient Word."

"Yes," a woman responded, "we allowed him to lead us down the path of darkness. We gave him power over us."

A nobleman also spoke. "We accepted his wars and his lies. We pretended not to see his decadence. We have created our own destiny."

"The destiny of the Toltecs was to rise to grandeur and splendor," a wise man said, "and so we did under the guidance of Quetzalcóatl. Now our Dear Prince is dead. Now our destiny is to disappear into the winds of time."

No one came to claim the body of the fallen Huémac, not his wife whom he had deserted, not his daughter whom he had misused, not Butterfly Woman. So the sorcerers delivered Huémac to the Land of the Dead. There they hung the battered body so the Fleshless Ones might see the remains of a worldly ruler who had made war instead of peace.

But the forces of destiny were not yet done. Quetzalcóatl, during his four-day sojourn in the Land of the Dead, came upon the tortured body of Huémac. There hanging on a lifeless tree was the once mighty leader of the Toltec Empire. Quetzalcóatl paused and looked at the body of the worldly ruler, and Quetzalcóatl wept, for in Huémac he saw his earthly image.

"Why do you weep?" Huémac asked.

"I weep because in you I see myself," Quetzalcóatl answered.

"We are not alike," Huémac said. "I chose the way of war and conquest. I was convinced that to make the Toltecs great I needed more land, wealth, and slaves. Now I see what I did on earth as a fitful nightmare. I thought I had to destroy you and everything you stood for, and for that I sold my soul to the gods of darkness. No, we are not alike."

"We are more alike than you think," Quetzalcóatl said. "You did not understand that all men have in their hearts the power to be great, the power of the quetzal bird to commune with the heavens. Each man is also rooted to the earth with feet of clay, and he is drawn to the wishes and desires of his blood. Each person is like the serpent who presses its body to Mother Earth, allied with that old memory of darkness. I am like this, my name also bears the name of serpent, *coatl*, the power related to the energies of the earth, to the instincts of reproduction and growth and death." ♥

"Quetzalcóatl, Lord of the Dawn," Huémac said after a long pause.

"When we first met, I told you my story. I am the Plumed Serpent, the Lord of the Dawn."

"And yet you came to earth, to Tollán. Why? Why here, at this time?"

"I came to bring art and civilization, a gift of Ometéotl, the Lord Who Created Mankind for His Pleasure. But to understand the heart of man, I had to take on the body of man. To redeem mankind, I had to fall."

"But we are not alike," Huémac insisted. As he spoke he groaned from the pain of death and from the thought that he would forever hang like a common thief from the tree in the Land of the Dead.

"We are like two sides of a coin," Quetzalcóatl said. "I saw that when we met. Our nature was one, but it was in conflict, it reflected the dual spirit of the universe. I could not conquer you, and you could not understand me. When you set out to destroy me, you were destroying yourself."

Huémac groaned. He understood now. "You only wanted to civilize us, to teach us a way to the eternal truth. . . . "

"Yes," Quetzalcóatl answered. "I wanted to show you how man may rise from the dust of the earth; through meditation, through prayer, through harmony and peace he may rise to greater levels of consciousness. I came to bring that knowledge to the Toltecs, to mankind."

Huémac twisted in pain. Now he understood, but it was too late. Then Quetzalcóatl cut down the body of Huémac, and he laid it in his own burial urn where it might rest. Even for this man who plotted his destruction, Quetzalcóatl had love. He had placed the dead body in the urn and wept for Huémac.

Ten

our days Quetzalcóatl dwelt in Mictlan, the Land of the Dead. He prepared arrows for his journey. On the eighth day he appeared, even as the morning star appears on the eighth day.

"It is time to journey to the east," Quetzalcóatl said to his attendants. "But first we must bury and conceal all the things we created. We must conceal all our wealth and treasures, conceal the beauty of my temple."

His attendants gathered all his wealth and hid it at a place called the Edge of Water, which was where Quetzalcóatl had bathed. No more would the people of Tollán see the beauty and wealth of Quetzalcóatl. The fabulous art of the Lord of the Dawn was hidden from all eyes.

It was the year One-Reed, exactly fifty-two years after his birth, that Quetzalcóatl left Tollán, seeking Tlapallan, the red land of the sun. They were ready to depart, seeking the sea of the east, seeking Tlillan, the Black Land, and Tlapallan, the Red Land, and Tlatlyan, the Fire Land.

But first he instructed his attendants to burn his house of gold and redshell, and his precious treasures were to be concealed in chasms within the mountain. Next he caused all the cacao trees to be changed into mesquite. He sent all the precious birds of Tollán ahead so they might meet him at Anáhuac, the eastern waters where his Father the Sun rose.

Now winter fell upon Tollán. It was a cold and bitter day when the people of Tollán gathered to see Quetzalcóatl begin his journey to the eastern waters. The people wept. Now truly, the glory of Tollán was ending. The people of Tollán wept because they would never see their Dear Prince again.

"I have visited the Land of the Dead," Quetzalcóatl said, "and now I journey to the eastern waters, there I will appear in my House Made of Dawn. There in the east I will spend my time, but one day I will return to you. As I was born in the year One-Reed, so I now die in the year One-Reed, and the fifty-two years of our sacred calendar are complete. I also vow to return in the year One-Reed, so at the end of every fifty-two year cycle you must await my return. I vow to return."

The people mourned, but they understood his promise. The Lord of the Dawn would rise each morning to light the way for his Father the Sun, and the light of the sun brought growth and energy. But no more would Quetzalcóatl the priest walk among the Toltecs. Now the only hope was that in the year One-Reed he would return, and so the sacred calendar of the Toltecs would be kept faithfully, the people would await his return. With this promise Quetzalcóatl departed.

From Tollán he traveled east, stopping first at Cuauhtitlán. There he saw his reflection in a stream and he said, "Truly, I have grown old." So he named the place Cuauhtitlán of Old Age, place of the Old Age Tree. He ceremoniously pelted the tree with stones, and the stones remained embedded in the tree.

Quetzalcóatl continued his journey. His attendants went before him, playing flutes to announce their master. When Quetzalcóatl sat to rest he saw in the distance the city of Tollán. Then he wept, and his tears fell as hail and pierced the rock on which he sat. When he leaned forward his hands made impressions in the rock. He called the place Temacpalco, the Place of the Handprints. Even today the indentations of the god can be seen there.

He arrived at Tepanohuahan, the Stone Bridge. There he built a stone bridge to cross the wide river. In his journey east he stopped also at Coahapan, the Water Serpent Place.

But even now as he marched eastward, the sorcerers would not let him rest. They appeared and blocked his way and tried to turn him back. They knew if he went to the land of his Father the Sun he would acquire tremendous power, and when he returned he would usher in a new time of wisdom and peace. "Where are you going?" the sorcerers asked. "Why are you leaving Tollán? Who will do penance if you leave?"

"I must leave Tollán," Quetzalcóatl answered.

"Where do you go?" the sorcerers asked, and Quetzalcóatl told them he was going east to Tlapallan.

"What business do you have there?" the sorcerers asked.

"I have been summoned by my Father, the Sun," Quetzalcóatl answered.

The sorcerers grew angry. They plotted to make Quetzalcóatl pay dearly for his faith in the path of light.

"Very well," the sorcerers said. "You may continue. But you must relinquish to us all of the Toltec arts."

Quetzalcóatl was too weak to stop them, and by force they took away all the arts. They took the art of casting gold, the art of cutting precious stones and jewels, the art of carving wood and working stone, the art of painting books and the art of weaving feathers. This was the cost they imposed on him before they let him pass; in this way the Toltecs lost their arts.

"You may have everything," Quetzalcóatl said. His time on this earth was done, and so he renounced the world. He cast his jewels and precious stones upon the water of the lake and they were swallowed up. He called that place Cozcahapan, Waters of the Jewels. Now it is called Coahapan, Water of the Serpent.

He traveled on, and another sorcerer came to meet him.

"Where you you going?" the sorcerer asked.

"I go to Tlapallan," Quetzalcóatl answered.

"Tlapallan, the place of light. But you cannot go there until you drink this magic potion I have prepared for you," the sorcerer said.

"No," Quetzalcóatl answered. "I must not drink it, I must not taste it."

"I cannot let you pass unless you taste it," the sorcerer said. "This is the magic drink which causes the mystic sleep. To enter your father's domain you must drink it. Otherwise I cannot let you pass."

Because he hungered for his father's presence, Quetzalcóatl drank the potion. He drank through a reed, and as soon as he drank it he fell asleep on the road. So he lost many days on the journey to his father.

When he awoke he felt refreshed. He arranged his long hair so he might continue his journey, and he gave the place the name of Cochtocan, Place Where Our Dear Prince Slept.

He continued, climbing between the snow-covered volcanoes, Ixtacihuatl and Popocatépetl, near Cholula. There it snowed and his servants froze. Quetzalcóatl was filled with grief, and he wept. He cried and sang the Death Chant.

These and many other places Quetzalcóatl visited as he journeyed eastward. The places where he visited and where he stopped are still marked, and people visit and pray there, for they are places of great power.

Now Quetzalcóatl turned away from death, he

turned to face the east. There he saw the snow-covered mountain, Payauhtecatl, home of the rain god, Tláloc, he who produces life. Here Quetzalcóatl made a wide turn, making a complete circle so he might see the land he was leaving, so he might move from death to life and be reborn again. From east to south he went, from south to the west, from the west to the north and then to the east again. In these four sacred directions he left his signs, and this is how the people knew he had been there.

At a certain spot on a mountain they say he frolicked and tumbled about like a trickster. He left the side of the mountain barren where he tumbled. He left a rope of maguey he used to pull himself up, and even today the people use the agave to make their fiber ropes. At another place he carved out a ball court as big as a canyon, and there he played the ball game the gods loved.

He found a giant ceiba tree, the tree which is the tree of life, and he shot one of his arrows through the heart of the tree. Then he himself passed through the tree whose sign was the cross, for the cross of the Tree of Life was the sign of Quetzalcóatl.

At another place he built an underground house, he built it like a tomb. He called the place Mitla, and it still exists near the village of the Oaxacan people. Still further on he erected a great stone in the shape of a phallus. This and many other things he did in the towns and villages of Mexico. They say he named all the mountains; everywhere he bestowed names.

For days he traveled, and yet no place was pleasing to him, for he was eager to greet his father. Finally he arrived at the sacred shore, the eastern waters of Tlapallan. He knew he had reached the place he was seeking, and he sat down and wept. Full of joy and full of misery was our Topiltzin Quetzalcóatl.

It was the year One-Reed when he reached the Celestial Water, the seashore where the sun rises. The water lapped the shore in the dark of night, and heavy was the gloom of night as Quetzalcóatl bathed himself and prayed. There he dressed himself in his glorious attire, his dress of the high priest of the Sun, with the bright plumes and turquoise mask. Now his glory was restored, now he was the strong and beautiful young Quetzalcóatl. The waters of the gulf lapped gently at his feet as he stood to face the east, and the dark waters took on a sheen of light. Oh, how beautiful was the Lord Quetzalcóatl in his attire of bright plumes!

There at the edge of the sea he commanded a raft of serpents to appear. Noble and proud he stepped on the litter towed by serpents, and he was carried away from the shore, over the gentle waters toward the place where the sun rises. His glory and nobility cast a light over the dark waters. Then as he prayed for the light of day to appear, a great fire consumed him and the Lord Quetzalcóatl surrendered himself to the fire of rebirth.

Thereafter, for all generations, the people would call that place Tlatlayan, the place where Quetzalcóatl became the shining light of the heavens, the place where he rose to announce the rising of his Father, the Sun. His story is still told by the people, they keep it in their hearts. In the year One-Reed, it is said, he will return. ❧

Glossary

This glossary was compiled to assist the reader in better understanding the Nahuatl terms and names used in this telling of the legend of Quetzalcóatl. I have used various sources to define these words; however, I do not claim the definitions are complete or comprehensive. The reader who is interested in the civilizations of Mesoamerica will go on to more extensive research and readings. Please use my glossary only to help you in understanding the story.

Anáhuac. Name applied to the Valley of Mexico, meaning "at the edge of the water" in Nahuatl. The Gulf Coast and the Pacific Coast also bore the name Anáhuac.

Aztecs. Belonged to the northern Uto-Aztecan language group. Legend tells us they left Chicomoztoc (Seven Caves) to begin their migration to the Valley of Mexico. They were composed of seven tribes, generally listed as the Acolhua, Chalca, Mexica, Tepaneca, Tlalhuica, Tlaxcalteca and the

Xochimilca. The aggressive Mexica conquered the Valley of Mexico by defeating the Tepaneca of Atzcapotzalco in 1428. By the time the Spaniards arrived the Aztec empire extended from the Gulf Coast to the Pacific Ocean.

Aztlán. The legendary land in northwest Mexico (or somewhere north of Mexico) where Chicomoztoc was located. It was the homeland or place of origin of the seven Aztec tribes.

Calmécac. A superior school where the most elevated aspects of Nahuatl culture were taught. Sons of kings, nobles and the rich attended, but apparently commoners could also send their sons to the calmécac.

Ce Ácatl Topiltzin. An early Toltec ruler who was born on the calendar day Ce Ácatl (One Reed). In about 980 he founded the Toltec capital of Tula. He was renamed Quetzalcóatl in his capacity as high priest of this ancient god of Teotihuacán.

Ce Ácatl. Means the year One Reed. It is also Quetzalcóatl's name. (The year One Reed occurred every fifty-two years. 1519, when the Spaniards landed in Veracruz, was the year One Reed, thus explaining the legend that Moctezuma thought Quetzalcóatl was returning to take possession of his Toltec kingdom.)

Ceiba. A sacred silk-cotton tree of Mesoamerica and of the Mayas.

Chinampa. "Floating gardens." Artificial islands built on the lakes around Tenochtitlán for agricultural purposes.

Cholula. Near the present-day city of Puebla, it was the most important center of the Mexican highlands after the fall of Teotihuacán. The pyramid there was dedicated to Quetzalcóatl and is the largest single structure in the New World.

Coatepec and **Zacatepec.** Places where battles took place. Coatepec was a dependency of the Acolhuacan state.

Eagles and **Jaguars.** Military fraternities. Their mystical origin relates to the sun (eagles) and the earth (jaguar). The warrior profession was esteemed, especially by the later Aztecs.

Huaxteca. (Or Huasteca.) A member of a cultural group living along the Gulf Coast and subject to Toltec authority.

Huémac. Reportedly the last king of the Toltecs.

Huitzilopochtli. An Aztec god of war and the sun, used in this telling of the Quetzalcóatl legend to signify the god of war and also the warring instinct of mankind. As one of the four primordial sons, (the Tezcatlipoca) Huitzilopochtli is the son of the creator pair Ometecuhtli and Omecíhuatl. In his capacity as sun he is daily born in the east and descends to the west to illuminate the underworld of the dead. As the god of war he was nurtured by the cult of human sacrifice.

Mictlan. The region of the dead, the hereafter. The land of the Fleshless Ones is ruled by Mictlantecuhtli and Mictlancihuatl, the Lord and Lady of the region of the dead.

Mimixoca. The four hundred, or countless, stars of the north, the luminous skirt of the feminine aspect of Ometéotl.

Nanahuatl. Or Nanahuatzin was the first god who threw himself into the fire at Teotihuacán to create the Fifth Sun, a new and present age. Perhaps it is from this myth that the Aztecs derived the need for human sacrifice so the sun and life could exist.

Nahuatl. The common language of the ancient Mexican Indian groups which settled in the great valley of central Mexico. The Aztecs, Cholulans, Chalcans and Tlaxcaltecs shared the Nahuatl language, traditions and ideas of the ancient Toltecs. The term Nahuatl came to be synonymous with the Aztecs because they rose to such great power.

Nahuatl century. Lasted fifty-two years. Each of the four directions was allotted a thirteen year period. In the tonalamatl (sacred calendar) there were twenty name days with the numbers one through thirteen to complete a year of 260 days.

Ometéotl. The god of duality. One of the most important concepts of Mesoamerica. Ometéotl was the Father (Ometecuhtli) and Mother (Omecíhuatl) of all the gods. He was known by many names and played a diversity of roles. Everything seemed to flow from Ometéotl, the foundation of the universe. In abstract thought he was the central androgynous godhead. [As "Lord of the Earth" Ometéotl was Tlaltecuhtli, his presence being in the naval (center) of the earth.]

Omeyocán. The supreme thirteenth celestial layer of the Aztec universe, and home of the divine pair, Ometecuhtli and Omecíhuatl.

Oxomoco. First woman and Cipactónal. First woman and first man. Were inventors of the calendar and astrology according to Toltec legend. Their myth links mankind's origin to the gods, that is to Ometeotl, the Lord of Duality. (In later versions Quetzalcóatl creates man and woman after his trip to Mictlan, again linking the creation to the gods.)

Pulque. An alcoholic drink fermented from the sap

of the maguey plant, its distillate is sold today as tequila.

Quetzalcóatl. The word takes part of its meaning from two words. Quetzal is the bird of bright plumage, therefore a creature of the sun. Cóatl means serpent, aligned to the reproductive, intuitive energies of the earth. The name fuses the two basic energies, that of the highest aspiration to the sun (godhead or the highest consciousness of mankind) and the serpent (creature of the earth). Quetzalcóatl was assigned one of the quadrants of the universe, ie., the energy of one of the sacred four directions. He was the foremost god of the Mesoamerican Indian pantheon, and creator of the Fifth Sun. The title Quetzalcóatl was also taken by the kings and high priests of the Toltecs.

Quetzalcóatl was worshipped in the guise of the Morning Star (Venus), hence his title Lord of the Dawn, a symbol of resurrection.

To omnipotence, Quetzalcóatl added the qualities of penance, mercy, humanity and civilization, characteristics imaged in Christ.

The Maya called him Kukulcán, the Quiche Maya called him Gucumatz. He was called the "feathered serpent" because he is portrayed as bearded. He was the god of learning and priesthood, source of agriculture, science, and the arts. He was linked to his human role through the legendary and historic figure Ce Ácatl Topiltzin Quetzalcóatl.

Quilaztli. Is Cihuacóatl or Coatlicue, "Lady of the Serpent Skirt" or "Snake Woman." (This could be Ometéotl in his maternal role. Also, Quetzal-cóatl—Cihuacóatl as creators of mankind were manifestations of the universal duality.)

Sun. Or Our Father the Sun, the giver of life. (Quetzalcóatl rises as Venus to light the way for the sun.) In more abstract terms, used in this story to signify the godhead, or Ometéotl.

Telpochcalli. The "house of young men" where the common people sent their youth for training, especially for warfare.

Tenochtitlán. The capital of the Aztecs. The Mexicas, one of the seven Aztec groups, lived on this island in Lake Texcoco. According to their myth the site was indicated to them by an eagle perched on a nopal cactus (tenochtli) with a snake in its beak. So, Tenochtitlán, today's Mexico City, was founded. The Mexicas combined with Texcoco in 1428 to crush the Tepanec empire, beginning the foundation of the Aztec empire.

Teotihuacán. Thirty miles north of Mexico City, it developed as one of the first urban centers of Mesoamerica from c. 100 B.C. to the seventh century A.D. This is one of the grandest sites in all Mesoamerica, containing some of the largest structures—the Pyramid of the Sun, the Pyramid of the

Moon, and the Pyramid of Quetzalcóatl. Destroyed around 650 A.D., this theocracy remains central to the study of Mesoamerica. The Toltecs borrowed much from the culture of Teotihuacán.

Tezcatlipoca. A creator god with many diverse forms. His name in Nahuatl means "smoking mirror." As god of night he was associated with deities of death, evil and destruction. He is associated with the material world as Quetzalcóatl is with the spiritual. In Toltec mythology he is an adversary of his brother Quetzalcóatl.

Tezcatlipoca is represented in directional colors as the Red Tezcatlipoca, associated with the east; Black Tezcatlipoca, "Smoking Mirror," warrior of the north; White Tezcatlipoca, "Plumed Serpent," Quetzalcóatl, associated with the west; and Blue Teacatlipoca, "Hummingbird Sorcerer," Huitzilopochtli, god of war and sun, associated with the south. The jaguar is the *nahual* of Tezcatlipoca.

Tláloc. God of rain. An aspect of Ometéotl in a life-giving role.

Tlamatinime. Wise men who taught a moral and judicial code of behavior.

Tlatlayan. The Fire Land.

Tlillan Tlapallán. Tlillan is the land of the black or

night. Tlapallán is the land of red or day, "land of sunrise" or the eastern coast where Quetzalcóatl went when he left Tula.

These lands merge in the west where the day ends, providing a mythical explanation of the death of the planet Venus when it sets in the west. Venus as morning star will reappear in the east, lighting the way for the sun which is the giver of life.

Tollán. The legendary capital of the Toltecs, present-day Tula. Founded by Ce Ácatl Topiltzin Quetzal-cóatl about 968 A.D. By 1,000 A.D. the city was a geopolitical centre of Mesoamerica. It collapsed in 1168.

Xochitlan. "Place of flowers", probably a chinampa.

Pronunciation Guide

The Aztec language, or Nahuatl, was spoken in Central Mexico, as well as in various parts of Central America, from Toltec times to the present. Written Nahuatl was transcribed into Latin by the Spanish missionaries after the Conquest, therefore it follows closely Spanish pronunciation.

a is pronounced as in father
e as in let
i as ee in knee
o as in lord
c is hard as in k, except when followed by e or i,
    then it is pronounced as in song
qu when preceding e or i sounds like k as in cover
z as in Sam
hu as w in want
tl and tz represent a single sound, tl as in rattler
x as sh in shoe

Most Nahuatl words are accented on the next to the last syllable. Accents are indicated today by accents used according to rules of Spanish accentuation.

CPSIA information can be obtained
at www.ICGtesting.com
Printed in the USA
LVHW051654070720
660006LV00003B/292

9 780826 351753